"In *Shiloh*, Fracassi's powerful, precise writing immerses the reader in the savage brutality of a Civil War battle – an exquisitely harrowing precursor to the strange horror of the tale. A masterful, mad charge into the weird." – Jeffrey Ford

"*Shiloh* gazes into the darkness and horrors of war and discovers an even deeper threat that dwells just beyond the veil of reality. Fracassi is a stalwart pioneer of the new weird and a literary cosmic voice whose originality goes unchallenged by few if any working in the field today. Not since Laird Barron came along have I seen an author so full of promise and potential." – Shotgun Logic

ABOUT PHILIP FRACASSI:

"…think vintage King at his best." — *Rue Morgue Magazine*

"Fracassi…builds his horrific tales slowly and carefully…his powers of description are formidable; and he's especially skillful at creating, and sustaining, suspense." — *The New York Times*

"This Fracassi guy is damn good." —Richard Chizmar, author of *A Long December* and co-author (with Stephen King) of *Gwendy's Button Box*

"Philip Fracassi is one of the most exciting new voices I've read…"— Ralph Robert Moore, author of *You Can Never Spit It All Out*

"I'm going to make a prediction here: Philip Fracassi will one day be one of the best and most well-known horror authors working in the genre… you need look no further than the work of this brilliant and rising star in the firmament of horror fiction." — Shane Douglas Keene, *Shotgun Logic*

"Philip Fracassi is the next big horror writer to blow your mind… If you're a fan of the horror genre at all, then this guy is a must-read." — Max Booth III

"Philip Fracassi is quickly building a reputation as a superior storyteller of incredible talent…. an author we must surely now hail as a leading light in the dark field of horror fiction." — Thomas Joyce

"Philip Fracassi is a master craftsman of the dark tale… a rare talent."–Paul F. Olson, author of *Whispered Echoes*

"…recalls the work of writers such as McCammon, King, and Bradbury." — *LOCUS Magazine*

"…one of the most promising and talented new horror authors to emerge in recent years." — RisingShadow.net

"Fracassi has a new fan. I'm going to be reading more of his stuff. You should, too." — Ray Garton

To McKinney —
Keep your head down!

SHILOH

by
Philip Fracassi

[signature]

Necronomicon '19

Lovecraft eZine Press

Copyright Philip Fracassi 2018

Front Cover Art by Heather Landry

Front Cover Design by Steve G. Santiago

Graphic Design by Kenneth W. Cain

Published by Lovecraft eZine Press

Formatting by Kenneth W. Cain

All rights reserved.

This book is licensed for your personal use only. No part of this book may be re-sold, given away, lent or reproduced to other parties by any means. Reviewers may quote small excerpts for their purposes without expressed permission by the author. If you would like to share this book with others, please consider purchasing or gifting additional copies. If you're reading this book and did not obtain it by legal means, please consider supporting the author by purchasing a copy for yourself. The author appreciates your effort to support their endeavors.

"Wings were growing on blistered feet. Bruised muscles and jolted bones...eyelids leaden from lack of sleep – all were pervaded by the subtle fluid, all were unconscious of their clay...If you had laid your hand in the beard or hair of one of these men it would have crackled and shot sparks."
– Ambrose Bierce

"And Elisha prayed, and said, LORD, I pray thee, open his eyes, that he may see. And the LORD opened the eyes of the young man; and he saw: and, behold, the mountain was full of horses and chariots of fire."
– 2 Kings 6:17

APRIL 6, 1862

THE FIRST DAY

I.

Pre-dawn.

I stare at a sky dark and blue as the men we are going to kill. The stars are spread across the fabric of night like spilled glitter, the moon's passive light blocked by the twisted veins of leaves above, the thick Spanish moss blackened window drapes, clinging to the sylvan arches of the surrounding skinny oaks. The air still chilled by the night, but warming. Our mother used to say that the hour before sunrise was the only time of day when the world was at peace. When man was closest to God. *Those serene moments, before the sun burns the horizon and opens its bright eye to stare judgment down on the wickedness of mankind,* she'd once said, holding our small hands on a dusty walk to church, *is when we are all momentarily innocent once more.* Amen, I guess. Although I feel none of the innocence she spoke of, despite the hour. The war might spare my life, but I'm confident my soul is long-since forfeit. You don't wash with another man's blood and expect to get clean.

William stands next to me among this cluster of tall trees, both of us Dixie Grey, both of us pumping Mississippi mud through our veins. His breathing is calm but I feel the tension coming off him, as I'm sure he can feel mine. Two brothers shoulder-to-shoulder, with another forty thousand brothers in arms extending in formation to each side, ahead and behind. The men ahead, the 1st Brigade under Russell, will be first to engage, for which I am thankful. All of us are exhausted beyond measure from an unrelenting two-day march up from Corinth toward Pittsburgh Landing, just shy of the mighty Tennessee River, our massive force trying to outmaneuver the North with speed and tactics, and hopefully numbers. We bivouacked near a white-washed church, but no one dared enter the structure. Our faith lies deep in Generals Johnston and

Beauregard, and our own Colonel Russell and Captain Smith. We don't have the weapons, and most of the men are inexperienced, but our leaders are smart, cunning, and tough. We'll win if we stick to the plan. Every man believes it as gospel.

    I force my thoughts to quiet, try to ready myself for what's coming. Dark lines of trees reach toward the Union-colored sky and I wonder if our grey army matches their wooden number, or if perhaps we have the advantage against this steadfast forest battalion. *If only we could fight the trees instead,* I think, and smile despite the cold moist air, my chilling fear. *Better them than the boys in blue up the river. And how do their numbers compare?*

    I decide to leave the answer alone. We'll know soon enough.

    I turn to William, nudge him with an elbow. His face, a reflection of my own, is buried in the shadow of a beaten cap, but his eyes are bright and his teeth shine in a malicious grin.

    "Stay close," I say under my breath, and his grin widens.

    "Always, brother," he replies wolfishly, then turns sincere. "Don't worry, Henry. They have no idea we're coming."

    I nod and start to reply in the affirmative – we hadn't seen a single blue vedette near our lines – when the snorting breath of a horse behind us breaks the serenity of the still, dark morning. We hear the harsh whispered commands of Captain Smith as he rides quietly down the line of men. "Muskets... muskets..." he says, drifting away into the dark, the word repeated in a dying echo. William and I remove bayonets happily. Our company was to be part of the next wave and we knew there'd be musketry, but we also knew that if we gained ground the fighting would be hand-to-hand – the bayonets and the fifteen-inch bowie knife strapped to my boot becoming the weapons of choice.

    William and I drop powder, ball and buckshot into our muskets and ram it home. I'm faster at loading than he is but for now we do our business in an unhurried fashion. No sense not doing it proper if you have the time. It will be different in the field, with artillery busting overhead and the Yankees shooting to kill, but for now we can be sweet about it. Nonchalant.

    I hear the company loading up, feel adrenaline steaming off nearby soldiers. The blood sings in every man, because in moments we will no longer be stationary, like the trees, but running, muskets at shoulders, aiming to kill and then some. We will become a wild hoard of murder breaking like a mighty wave over those damned bluecoats. Those would-be usurpers of Lincoln.

The trees grow lighter. I make out patterns in their bark. Down past my brogans I study the earth beneath me. I expect dead grass and mud. I see violets instead. Purple and bright. Life. The other men look around as well, as if waking up. The sun is coming. The dawn is dying. The day is here.

Shots ring out.

William looks at me, eyes wide and terrified. Anxious. My younger brother by a few minutes, identical in near every way. But now he looks mad. Likely, we all do. Half the men grin nastily through their beards and I realize I'm grinning, as well.

"Get ready," I say, no longer needing to whisper. Bullets whizz by our ears like hornets, tap into the branches above our heads.

In the enemy camp, bugles sing, fill the lightening air. Union horns call their boys to assembly. We can hear the cheers.

More musket-fire. Both sides now. Horse hooves beat into the ground behind us but I stare steadfastly forward. Focus on the tree before me – there's a shape in the bark that makes me think of a face with a mouth stretched too long, a hollow scream.

There's a *ping* and a thud only inches away, as if someone's struck the tree with a hammer. Chips of bark fly at our faces. William looks at me, as if surprised, eyes saucer-wide.

"Can you believe this shit?" he practically yells, looking as if he might bust into wild laughter. "They're shooting at us!"

I laugh, as do a few of the others. William's voice is deeper than mine and has a sharp southern twang, which sells his sense of humor. I was never very funny, and I talk too quiet. Mother says it's the mark of a Southern Gentleman, but I think it's just that I'm more shy than little brother. Than most, I guess, although not so much anymore. War has a way of pulling wallflowers off the paper, forcing them into the garden, stuck there to live or die.

Horse beats pound closer and the command can't come soon enough. "Forward march!" Smith yells, and you hear the same command echoed, like the enemy's bugle call, all through the trees and into the soft valleys. Down the line.

I reckon it's near five in the morning when we start to walk forward, muskets pointed. We slip past trees but stay in formation. As we move through the forest – ever nearer the wild plain and the Union camps – we can hear the battle approaching, coming close to meet us. More shots come at us now, the Union men firing wildly into the trees, and I almost sense their disorganization and alarm, their fear and excitement. A cannon coughs and I am surprised, their battery being organized so quickly is not a good sign for us. But no time now, no time left for worry, as our pace quickens. The battlefield is coming into view, the trees alive with bullets tearing and punching at leaves and branches, spitting into the trunks with sick thuds that come so steadily it makes me wonder for a moment how I'm still alive.

Before us is a churning sea of grey on a carpet of green. Sheets of blue smoke and the blistering repeating taps of shots fired hang over the boxes of soldiers before us as they move steadily forward, toward the frantically assembling Union camp. Flashes of blue uniforms in the distance. Running men falling into great lines. Artillery being rolled into place. A flag waves from a high pole. Vast rows of humped tents roll up the slope in merciless numbers and precise lines. All of it is filtered in shadow, the veil of the dying dawn, but coming to life, the shapes of tents and men edged by shimmering light as the red sun breaks between a cleft of green hills, lighting the world on fire. A newborn god of war given frantic birth.

A few feet from me someone screams and a body drops.

"Ready!"

The Captain yells but it's hard to hear because the noise is growing. The musket-fire is now constant. The trees pop and spit wood chips at us as minnies tear into our positions. Another man in my peripheral vision is knocked backward and I have time to see a mist of red hanging in the air when the order is thankfully given. I point my weapon and line my shot: A bluecoat standing in formation, white face under a jostled cap, his own musket seemingly pointed directly at me.

"Fire!"

I pull the trigger in time with a hundred others and the eruption splits my hearing, a ringing deep in my head that's temporarily louder than the shots and cries. I spend only a moment relishing the sight of my target dropping to his knees, clutching madly at his neck. I want to believe I can see his blood. We're all reloading, and now men are taking cover behind this last line of trees before we break into the open. Something hits me hard in the face and for a moment I panic, reach my cheek and see blood on my fingers.

"Jesus Christ," I say and William, kneeling behind a tree only half his width, looks up at me in a panic. He sees my face then smiles, points to my shoulder. My hand reaches up and pulls away a thick branch that had been broken by gunfire and fallen like a chopping axe, swiping my skin in the process. Not shot, then. But wounded.

And what an ever-loving relief it is. First blood, and now I am liberated. No longer invincible. I'm ready to run wild, to toss down my musket and attack Grant himself with nothing but my knife and a mad lust for glorious death.

"It's getting warm!" someone yells, and now we all find targets once again. More men cry out and fall but it doesn't matter, there are too many of us, tens of thousands, and we are ready to swarm.

"Fire!" comes the repeated command and again we fire in unison. This time my target is a youthful Aide on horseback. I miss the boy but hit the horse, or so I think because it buckles and the rider is thrown. I pray for his neck to be broken.

"Bayonets! Bayonets!"

I pull the bayonet from my belt and, in a smooth practiced motion, affix it with a push and tightening twist. Men are yelling, being held back now by a thread, the bloodlust pumping in our ears, eyes wide with adrenaline. The few thousand men already on the field are breaking toward the camp. Oh glory! *Jesus Captain!* I think. And then...

"Double-quick!" comes the command and we break from the trees like a wrathful horde of mythic beasts. Thousands of us scream and the power of that scream blunts the sounds of musket-fire and artillery, overwhelms and overpowers it all. My mind snaps, perhaps, in that instant and I am truly mad, feral and wild. There are waves and waves of us breaking free into the open, and all the men yell at the top of their lungs, louder than the horns of heaven and meaner than the hounds of hell come the Dixie Greys and the Volunteers who support us. Nothing can stop up from taking the field, not ship or cannon or God himself. As we scamper up the rise behind the 1st Brigade, the way is clear. We've driven them back with little effort, the surprise attack a success.

We breach the camp's edge and the bluecoats are running, and I like to think it's Sherman's horse at a gallop in front of the Yankee backs. I side-step an abandoned cannon and stomp through a smoldering fire pit. A skillet rests on a charred stone, blackened meat and beans steaming inside. A breakfast disrupted by war.

I lower the point of my bayonet as we walk urgently past tents and strewn clothing. A soldier at my side cries out a warning and I watch with amazement as a naked boy springs from the mouth of a tent and runs straight toward me. I run him through the guts as another stabs him through the side of his pale chest, snapping ribs. We pin him to the ground and I pull free, stick him again in the heart and again in the face. I kick his shocked mouth with the heel of my boot, still warm from tromping through the fire, and would spit in his watering eyes had I the time, for our line is still moving, forward, forward.

"They fly!" a soldier yells out.

The cry is taken up by more men, and our shouts crescendo, a cloudburst of cheers. It seems the whole world screams in mad joy.

The stragglers of the Union brigade – the over-sleepers and the ill-prepared – are shot or run-through or taken prisoner if an officer is present. I'd wager we kill a thousand or more. Bodies are dense. I step through more than one pool of blood traversing the site, looking for survivors, souvenirs. I stride past a Volunteer pissing on a dying man, whooping and thrilled to still be alive. Others are scavenging tents and packs for food, hardtack most likely, or clothes, new boots or weapons. Most of us press forward up the rise, a venomous deadly grey swarm sweeping over the hill like locusts. We have taken the first camp and now look toward the distant swell of the Tennessee River riding northeast, where Grant waits with another twenty thousand men. A copse of dense forest sits just north; a soft valley settles to the west. A second camp is ahead, through the trees and a series of deep ruts, and that is where we must march. There is a road that bends round, and some structures can be glimpsed, but we want the cover of the trees so into the thick we'll go. Besides, time is our enemy. Buell is en route with a division, maybe two, and we have but a day to break Grant and push his men back into the waters of the big river, hold the South. Having just lost Kentucky and Tennessee, a line has been drawn that we must hold. I worry, however, that this initial battle has been too easy, made the men too eager. We caught them unawares but that won't happen twice. We won't be waking men up with a bayonet through the eye. They'll be ready.

William stands with his arms raised above his head, bellowing in victory. Somehow his face had been misted with blood and it makes his eyes shine white and large as the rising sun bathes the scene in yellow and shows us all the glory of our early triumph.

II.

Our division forms up at the north edge of the overrun Union camp. Seems Russell is gonna drive us right up Sherman's asshole on this next push, while Hardee and those boys drive Grant toward the river. The men are ready. My hands are shaking, not from fear but anticipation. I want to kill more Yankees, and the morning is warming up; my legs and back already run with sweat.

The regiment moves into the thicket. The earth here is soft and hard to find footing, the sun once again broken into shadows by draping moss and skyward-reaching trees. William and I are separated, but I can see him twenty men down the line. I wonder if his distance is an awareness of our ferocity or just plain shame. I reprimanded him briefly for looting, not because I care about a dead Federal soldier's belongings, but because the lines were fraying. Men were pulling blackened meat from warm skillets, pulling boots from corpses and corpses-to-be, and some were trying to walk the opposite way, back toward the South, arms filled with clothes and other booty. One of these men was shot by Brigadier General Hindman, and that turned the rest around. The Union is organized, well-supplied, experienced. Veterans. If the Confederates are going to match them, we need to be on point, and I told William as much in a heated manner. He only laughed, rubbed at the back of a watch he'd found, and walked away.

Many of the men found further resolve at seeing the battery push in behind us. Four horse-pulled cannon and a hundred men to handle them. The limbers were cracked and blackened, but those six and ten-pounders would do a fine job. Their shot will blast through a line of men and send them flying like dandelion seeds caught in a gust of hot wind.

We're ordered to slow our pace, and I hunch, step carefully around trunks and bushes. Insects buzz in my ears, and I find myself once again awaiting entrance into the clearing, to see the elephant head-on. I worry about William, about my dying and leaving him here alone. I look down the line to find him, but the trees are too dense. Next to me, a boy is crying, breaking thoughts of my brother and what lies ahead.

"You a Dixie Grey or a Volunteer?" I ask, knowing the answer.

"Vol," he says, and moans when his shoe sticks into mud. He pulls it free with a squelch and the bottom peels down like an open mouth, the toes within black as the worn-out leather.

Ahead of us are shouts. Artillery is fired from a distance, and I curse, knowing damn well that the second camp is reinforced and ready to meet our front.

There's a whistling and something breaks through the trees behind us. A thud like a bass drum and the ground shakes. A wave of heat singes the nape of my neck. The kid cries out and throws down his gun, which I notice to be nothing more than a boy's hunting rifle, not long ago used for shooting pheasant versus man. I begin to speak when the trees in front of us blow apart; a wall of leaves and timber disintegrate before our eyes. The world fills with thunder and an erupting barrage of gunfire the likes I've never heard in my short time as a Confederate.

"Lie down!" someone yells, the command barely audible in the deadly chaos. Grape shot blows through trees and bodies like grains of sand in a desert storm. I turn and grab the boy's collar, readying to shove him face-down into the mud. His pale face pops open like a pimple and ragged chunks of his cheeks and brow and lips jerk into red jelly as bullets punch into his head. I push the thin corpse away in horror and drop to the earth, hands over my cap, lips and teeth pressed hard into mud and leaves and bugs. I realize I'm screaming and make myself stop, but my breath still comes in quick ragged hiccups of shock and fear, and I pray the trunk of the tree just past my crown will survive the deluge and keep me whole. I think that I'd love to see the sunset one more time, that I'd like to see the moon in the sky and feel the cool night air. Please God let this be a memory, and not the present.

The fighting is everywhere, the battle officially underway after our preemptive strike. There are booms and cracks from the valley to the left, heavy detonations of Union fusillade and broken screams mixed with distant cheers toward the river to my right. Our single line, extending a mile or more, likely getting decimated by the Union artillery and, closer to the Tennessee, the gunships. There's the slightest slowing from the non-stop shatter of bullets around me, and I nearly cry out when a heavy weight falls on my back.

"Henry!"

I twist my face but dare not lift my head. William's own grinning visage meets me. He has a slice running the length of his forehead but his eyes are alive and vibrant.

"I just heard!" he yells into my ear, the words dulled despite his being inches away. "Our battery is set. We're not to move."

He laughs, hysterically I think, but his mouth is no longer smiling. It's the laugh of disbelief, of a kind of madness.

I don't reply because I fear moving even an inch lest my teeth catch a bullet, but as if on cue our cannons bellow from behind and somewhere adjacent, outside the trees. Two batteries then! My imagination paints a picture of long-cannon firing great gouts of grape shot and shells into a field of blue men, tearing them to ribbons. Behind us, the mortars. Their magnificent barks bring me to my senses, restore my bravery. In my head, I know we throw the same metal at them as they do us, but when I know those soaring shells are sent fly from Confederate steel I can't help but feel they're louder, more powerful, and more deadly than the enemy's.

A moment passes, and the competing volleys of bullets slow to an uneven trickle. I hear cheers from the line and dare to lift my head. Other men are standing. Beyond the trees, there are yells of chaos. A command comes down the line.

"Forward! Forward!" someone yells from my left – not my captain, not a voice I recognize. But I'm standing, my brother beside me once more. I'm trembling, my teeth chatter despite the warming day. I stare in disbelief.

It's the trees. They're all but gone. Torn to stumps, branches swaying, broken and torn. I can clearly see the second Union camp ahead, because our cover has been blown away. Smoke billows to the West, and I realize that the trees are burning.

"Is your musket loaded?" I ask, and William nods, raises the stock to his shoulder.

"Forward!" the men cry out. As one, the line begins walking through the decimated thicket.

We go steady and enter the clearing, the glorious battleground. A line of grey stretches east and west. Blue lines are breaking but determined. There are lines upon lines of them, and it seems our brigade is but one stretch of grey string, hoping not to be cut to pieces.

A cry goes up. The battle to the east is fierce, and a rider and his steed are driving for it. The men roar, their cry filled with ferocious pride, for the rider is our own General Johnston. The greatest commander in the South. I watch him as he passes, not fifty paces from our line, like a bullet of grey steel shot from a gun. I can make him out well enough to see blood flowing from his leg, but he seems undaunted and ready for whatever may come.

There is something else, and I fear deep in my heart I am the only one who sees it... I don't want to believe.

Despite how I was raised, I hold no faith in most things. Our daddy, you see, was a preacher. Died from pneumonia when William and I were still getting by with crawling, contracting the virus after spending the majority of a frigid morning dunking parishioners in purifying waters, more commonly known, especially by those trolling for catfish, as Black Creek. As we grew older and became aware of the significant void in our lives, Mother comforted us by saying our daddy died saving souls. Regardless, neither William or I had much to do with religion once it was understood to be the thief who stole our father away in the night. Seemed ridiculous to pray to an uncaring God. No point begging to an almighty being if we all ended equal. In the dirt. Mother liked to tell us about the afterlife, about heaven. About streets of gold and angels playing harps and cities in the clouds, but I know bullshit when I hear it, and it doesn't have to be stuck to my shoe for it to stink.

Point being I don't hold stock in these ideas. Fairy tales and Bible verses are one and the same to me.

So you can imagine my bewilderment and horror at seeing a demon incarnate on the battlefield, riding horseback through the tumult and carnage behind the great General Albert S. Johnston, ripping at his back with whip-fast claws, pulling long strings of frayed black substance from the great man who, for all the veracity of the creature's devilish work, seems none the wiser to its relentless attack upon his non-corporeal self.

I don't know what it means. Why the vision comes to me now. Perhaps I have truly gone insane, or perhaps it is a vision from an unlikely God. The only thing I know for certain – and it is a truth so hard and unarguable as the sky being up and the earth being below – is that the great General Johnston is a dead man.

He just doesn't know it yet.

III.

Despite my earlier protestations, William and I are among the scavengers of the second massive encampment. Now that we've taken the ridge, and the immediacy of the battle has temporarily waned for our company, I can't begrudge the logic of stopping to savor the spoils of conquest.

Besides, we are hungry, and the army is in short supply of food. It's impossible to suggest men pass up the bounty found among the tents and fire pits of the Union camp. The river runs in the distance, and the fortifications of Pittsburg Landing by Grant's men stand at the ready. They appear as long lines of dark blue scratched into earth, as if drawn there by the Yankee God in jagged ink.

Lieutenants, and even a colonel or two, attempt to rally our regiment, but all I see are soldiers wolfing down scraps of meat, hardtack, discarded apples. A few of the men are singing *Peas! Peas! Peas! Peas! Eating goober peas!* as they kick corpses and rummage through bloody blue pockets. One of the Volunteers shoots another over a treasure – a clamped pot of stew. The Vol is subsequently manacled and taken to the rear, where they'll most likely kill him or set him on his way, marked as a deserter. William finds a sack filled with carrots and bread. We sneak into a hot dark tent and devour it all, ready to kill anyone who enters without our leave, or god forbid makes for our prize.

I'm still haunted by the image of the demon, clutched to the general like a hideous vulture pulling the innards of his soul free, but have made peace with it and call it what it is: a delusion. Shock. My mind's way of dealing with the horror and hunger and exhaustion of the day and the days that came before it.

And it has truly been a horrifying day. Just past noon and already thousands dead. Most of the wounded have been left among the burning trees, or face-down in the marsh. Several Union officer's tents of the southern camp have been made into Confederate field hospitals, the tents nothing more than a butcher's meat grinder, the surgeons inside twirling machinations of metal that pull the limping, bleeding and wounded into the front and spit pieces of men out the back –

arms and legs and corpses – thrown into an already overflowing ditch dug by other men who will likely soon help fill it. Along with my brother and I, to be sure.

A thunderclap breaks overhead but I hardly notice as it fits in so perfectly with the foregoing thunder coming from the river. We've heard word that the gunships are hunkered in beneath the shoreline and can fire at our positions all day and all night without fear of retaliation, and so they have done. The earth constantly trembles, the air scorched. My teeth vibrate in my head and my ears are near deafened by the constant barrage on the senses.

The big fear among the men is that Grant has reinforcements coming in, and we've only a few hours to settle the matter. Our brigade is to push the blues back and north, let our other brigade toward the east push the Union away from the river, cut them off from supplies and crush them between us. There are not many roads left to use, however, and if we're going to break through it'll be by way of a sunken road, an offshoot of the mighty river, now dry enough to use as a pass, straight to the heart of the bastards.

Despite the officers' best efforts, it isn't until we hear the cry of Union bugles and the screams of terror outside our current position that we drop our looting to ready for arms. William and I burst from the tent to a scene from Hell itself – grey uniforms in hasty retreat, running back toward the trees and the first overrun camp. To the northeast the blues are surging, and our men scramble to form ranks.

"Muskets!" comes the cry and we fire at will. One of our batteries has pushed up and now blasts straight into the Federals, forcing their lines to stagger. I ram another ball into my barrel and let out a bloody scream. William joins me and soon other men rally to formation. We walk steadily toward the Union lines that are now pulling away, back toward that sunken road. We push them a hundred yards, straight east, away from the camp. More greys form a line to the west. We will meet at their heart and crush them.

Murderous cries come from the right as a line of hidden blues burst from the trees, bayonets level, and charge our battery.

They go for our cannons.

The surprise attack shakes us, and a few men drop guns and run. I charge.

Two companies in total fling themselves against this

new Union attack. Without our artillery, we're doomed and we damn well know it. I don't recognize half the men with me anymore and I'm not sure who is giving orders, but instinct takes over and you do what must be done. If a knife is being plunged toward your foot, you do not turn a blind eye, you pull your boot back to defeat the stabbing blow.

I fire a shot into the back of a hatless soldier and pause only to fix my bayonet. The field has become a brawl. William runs on without me, right into the fray. Yelling incoherently, beyond my senses, I leap into the mix.

I run my bayonet through the chest of a grizzled Yankee. Something punches the side of my head, my ear pops and rings, my mind flickers and I drop to a knee. I find the strength to gain my feet, am deep within the skirmish when my eyes deceive me again. It's a whirlwind of grey and blue, the spurting, showering red of blood everywhere. A bluecoat is strangling one of our battery men who stabs his side mercilessly with a blade. Some Federals are stabbing a horse to death with bayonets. The great beast screams and topples drunkenly onto its side. A Dixie Grey staves off two Union soldiers with the barrel of an empty musket, swinging it like a club, but he is quickly overtaken and slaughtered as he shrieks for mercy.

I see all this, as if time is slowed, but I also see, as opaque as flesh, the demons running rampant throughout. They leap from man to man, pulling at their substance, their bodies covered in gore and shadow, despite the unfiltered sun overhead. Thunder rumbles again and I look to the heavens. I squint at a bright light, a white hole in the sky. The light ignites the skirmish with white brilliance, and the demons evaporate, leaving only the human killers behind to fight.

There's a crack so loud it feels the world is breaking, like the dome of sky has broken in two. The ground shakes and I lose my footing. A few of the fighting soldiers notice the tumult and one gets a saber through the middle when he looks around for the source. A musket cracks and William is thrown backward.

"Will!" I scramble on hands and knees toward him, pulling my knife free of my boot as I do. An old soldier in blood-stained blue stands over him, rams downward with the point of his bayonet and my brother screams. I snarl and leap at the soldier, jam my blade through the side of his neck and land atop him as he crumbles. I pull the blade free and a wash of warm blood shoots from his gouged throat and over my hand

and forearm. I spin to William, see his eyes open and searching. A hot bullet has sliced open his scalp cleaner than a Cherokee blade. A flap of skin reveals the dull white of skull above his temple, but I don't see his brain and I thank my mother's soul for this. Far worse than the damage done by the bullet is the stab wound. It punched through his belly below the ribs and sliced sideways, opening his stomach. Dark blood pumps through the slit in his shirt and I know the gash is deep, likely fatal.

Ignoring the fight, I round and grip him under the arms, drag him back toward the tree line where the blues had been hiding in wait.

Deep enough where he can lay unseen, I rest him in the cool shade of the trees. He coughs and blood splatters his lips. I kneel beside him, take off my jacket and hold it to the wound in his stomach, leaving be the scorched bullet trail alongside his head until I slow the bleeding in his guts.

There are insects all around, swarms of them. They settle on my perspiring neck and face, buzz in my ears. They land on William's chest and face, crawl on his eyes, but I can do nothing at the moment except press into his sliced stomach. I can do nothing but think of saving my twin brother's life.

Behind me, the battle growls and snaps, explodes and howls, but it is all distant. A memory. If I can't save William, then the battle is irrelevant, because it is already lost.

Orders are cried out; lines are reforming. Voices come closer, yelling for me to rank up. Will's breathing is shallow, and he grips my sleeve with white knuckles.

"I must attend," I say, and pull myself free. I leave my coat. "Press on this. I'll be back." Hurriedly, I bury him to the neck. Leaves and dirt and mud over his legs and arms. I tuck the musket beneath him. I pile leaves around his head. "If these trees catch fire, you'll need to crawl clear."

He nods sickly as I gather my weapon and leave him to the trees, start for the cluster of men closest to me. None of the faces are men I know. I turn back once more, can just make out my brother's beard and sun-reddened eyes through the shadowed leaves.

A man stands over him.

I cry out, begin to break rank, return to his side and protect him, but pause. This man, this giant, seems to be doing nothing more than studying my brother, his posture passive, his head cocked. The massive brute, the tallest I've ever seen, is naked, but somehow not exposed. His skin, though smooth, seems strong as hard leather, beneath which muscles flex and ripple like melting iron. He holds a spear the length and girth of a ten-year-old pine, the tip, a gleaming metal, appears savage, deadly. There is a glow coming off him that is near blinding.

I can look upon him no longer. My eyes already run wet, my skin hot, my scalp burning. I wipe my cheek with the back of a hand and feel nothing to see it smeared with warm blood. I am shaking with fear that I have turned mad, and refuse to look back again. Instead, I run toward the men, already pressing forward.

The word has come down. The Union holds a position of strength that keeps the main body of our army from reaching Grant, pushing his men into the swamps and finishing them. Our company forms quickly with three others, not nearly a regiment but we have a Brigadier General forming our lines nonetheless. A man named Wood, who rides around us barking like a dog herding scared cattle, pushing us through the chute into whatever lies beyond. Our formations are so tight my toes are bumping the heels of the man before me as we march northeast.

The land dips but we stay on high ground, though the slanted terrain makes it difficult to remain in clean lines. Dead stumps the size of carriages stick from the earth, trees of all shapes and sizes sprout in makeshift clusters. There are a million places for a man to hide in ambush, and we pray the scouts who've run ahead are keen-eyed and not throat-slit.

The artillery barrage from both sides has yet to cease, or slow. The bludgeoning is so commonplace now that it goes hardly noticed. Smoke floats through the trees that are starved of leaves, stark as forked lightning, grey and streaked in blue-black mist. They remind me of Baptists raising their hands praising Jesus in a burning church.

The man before me curses as he stumbles over a body, falls to a knee. He resumes and I step over the corpse, but there are too many on the ground and the ranks fragment, bending around bodies and stumps and bramble as we push on. Ahead is the spatter of fired muskets.

"Briskly forward, if you please!" Wood yells, and the men – somehow not dispirited by the ghastly surroundings and steady litter of fallen men and bloodied horses they must step over and around – give a replying cheer and increase their pace. My musket is rammed and loaded. We enter a thick grouping of dark trees, see vertical streaks of blue ahead. The air around me and the men is a greenish-yellow, like candlelight underwater. An explosion punctures the earth ten yards ahead and I'm sprayed with dirt.

"Double-time! Form a line through the trees!"

I scream because I'm terrified, scream to give myself courage. My lungs are raw, and I bolt forward, dodging trunks and branches to gain the clearing, ready to kill. The men surrounding me are also screaming, cursing, praying as they run. We break through the tree-line and I gasp, the world open before me. "Oh shit," I say, momentarily stuck. For the first time, I see the full scale of it. The glory of the battle.

A vast field is laid out ahead, a road dips to the right, trailing toward a thick vein of blue – the Tennessee. It's the closest I've been. In the distance are charcoal boats on the river, tens of thousands of blue dots ready to fight line the banks. Smoke trails from encampments, the whole of mankind shooting and dying. The sky is smattered with puffs of black smoke, pounding cannons shake the earth.

Bullets sizzle by my head and I raise my musket.

"Hold!"

The men form a line, muskets at their shoulders, finding targets. A company of blues come at us, precise in their movements, like figures made of clockworks instead of blood and meat. I envy their order, their control.

A bark of an order from their line and muskets lower into place. Shoulder-height.

We wait, hold steady. Discipline reigns even though it seems these Federals all aim for my skull, a hundred rounds ready to tear me from life.

They fire. I hear lead smack meat and know men are dying, but make myself still, like a statue. Hidden from death by my cold heart. Slowly, as if he's fallen asleep, the man in front of me slumps backward, his head bumps against my chest as he falls, his pale face turned toward heaven. The blues reload, march closer, closer. Fifty paces divide us.

"Hold!" Wood bellows. "Hold 'til you see the whites of their teeth!"

The soldier next to me is crying. I turn to him. His fevered eyes catch mine.

"Get ready to catch hell," he says, and the blues fire.

Behind me more Dixie-Greys march into formation. I feel pride and amazement. Pride in my army, amazement that I'm still alive.

I think about William, and hope he's alive as well.

The blues are close. I see their teeth.

"Fire!"

A third of our company is dead, but those who remain tear apart the Federal line. All but a handful are blown backward, or drop. A man's hand is shot clean off, another's face flowers red. The boy I target catches it in the belly. He leans on his musket like an old man might put his weight on a cane. The Brigadier General yells for bayonets but I'm already running, sprinting and howling forward to pull the wounded boy's fucking guts out. I drop my musket and free my knife from the strap in my boot without breaking stride. I don't know if other men follow me. My only care is this boy and his guts. My eyes and mouth are wide and I'm singing in my head, a hymnal or a symphony I don't rightly know. I want to sink teeth into the young soldier's neck. Within two feet, he tries to raise his unattached bayonet and I swat it aside and drive my blade into his sternum. We both go down and I sink my teeth into his meaty, shaven cheek as he screams. I rip flesh free and spit it onto his face, then straddle him at the thighs and saw my blade downward, sternum to groin, splitting him. I shove my hand inside and it's like a bath of blood eels. I grab one and pull it free, throw it to the side, pull a few yards more before I realize his eyes are empty, the heart still.

I wipe my blade on his chest and sheath it, turn and look for my musket. Greys run past me, into the thick of the hornet's nest beyond.

I see more demons among them, all black as night. One has horns that spiral high and twisting over its head. One wears the gray poncho of a fallen soldier like a cape, while another flies like a crow, weaving between men. I stare too long at the horned creature and am noticed. White eyes stare back, flicker red and yellow. I catch a glimpse of its face – a mouthful of teeth, a wet snout. I look away, look down. I find my musket in the mud, lift it free, pause, then walk away from the battle. Back toward the thicket, the spot of ambush, and my brother.

A second regiment steps through the trees, spread a thousand yards across, heading toward the field, toward possible victory. Covered in gore, I walk straight through them. Two soldiers move aside to let me pass. Neither look at me.

"Catch hell, boys," I say, and continue alone toward my twin. One of the men turns before I'm out of range. "Hey," he yells, words clear despite the sounds of battle surrounding us. "Johnston's dead!"

I go around the trees, down and up through a ravine. I'm forced to skirt a small pond, and wonder if I've lost my sense of direction. The pond is thick with shocks of hair, uniforms and blood. The water deep red. Thunder erupts again and this time the clouds break.

By the time I reach the war-torn patch of land where I buried my little brother, I'm soaked through.

APRIL 6, 1862

NIGHT

I.

I find William at dusk. Twice I am forced to change my path and take cover from Union artillery. I crest the ridge and look over that morning's battlefield. I spy the camp we took in the late morning. There are no fires to draw attention but there is the movement of shadows among the tents. The sun is settling into the horizon. There's so much smoke in the air that the sky is red as blood. The land itself is an image of Hell. There are fires spreading through trees, adding biblical texture to the infernal landscape. The ground is littered with bodies, blue and grey. Some lie still, some crawl. Some moan at me when I pass, begging for water, for food, for help. If I counted them all I'd go mad, but my estimate is a few thousand dead and dying lay wasted across the scope of my vision.

I try to move faster, worried that Will is dead or caught in a fire, but my body is spent and bruised and empty. The tip of my musket drags a line in the dirt as I walk, a path for those who would follow.

By the time I locate Will, the red sky has gone plum, the air chilled by the night's shattering rain, now slowed to a drizzle. A sticky mist. Despite the dark and the weather, the cannonade has not slowed. The sounds of battle between infantries, at least, has waned with sun's light. Overhead, artillery trails scratch the heavens, the torn celestial flesh oozing fire.

I don't know how far the army pushed forward, if they backed the blues into the river or beyond, or if the Union had time to fortify. Tomorrow, I know, will decide it all. If the Union gets more men, they'll gun us down like dogs. If not, if we have one more day, I know in my heart we can whip them. Johnston was a great general, but Beauregard will step in ably, and he is more aggressive than Johnston. He'll order every last man forward, forward... until we are all victorious, or we are, each of us, dead.

II.

William is unmoved. William is alive.

I push the leaves away from his head, sweep the dried clumps of dirt off his legs and arms. I put a hand on his cheek and speak his name.

His eyes open and find me. He smiles. A thrill goes through me, a song plays fast-tempo in my veins and the weight of ten men falls from my shoulders.

"What the hell you smiling about?" I say, not able to contain the giddiness of my voice, the raw hope.

"I'm feeling alright," he says.

I shake my head and my smile falters. *He must be in shock,* I think. *He's probably so close to death as to be numb to the pain.*

"Well, that's a good thing, ain't it," I say, and he nods more vigorously, with more strength in him than I would have thought possible. "Okay, take it easy. Let me have a look."

I take his hand off my blood-soaked jacket and lift it gently away from the wound, but at an angle, so that he won't see the damage.

"My God!" I say, so loudly that it breaks the sanctuary of the night, shatters the invisible temple of us. I drop the jacket back down and fall onto my rear, my hand to my mouth in shock. He looks at me, concerned, frightened. I stand up and begin to pace. William follows me, eyes nervous, mouth twitching.

"Is it bad, Henry?" he says, and then he swallows and his face tightens with determination. I love him more in this moment than I ever have. "I'm not afraid to die!" he yells into the night, defiant.

"I don't know," I stammer. "It's not bad... I don't know what the hell it is."

He says nothing, and makes no move to touch the jacket. He looks away from me, as if wanting to be alone with his thoughts, and that's when I notice his head. The flap of skin has been put back into place, and the wound glows green, a luminescence so bright it smears light onto the surrounding earth, the jagged, broken trunks of nearby trees. I feel its shine on me. My skin prickles with it, my eyes absorb it like dew. A tightness in me softens, the sting in my eyes lessen, then disappear. I'm refreshed, as if I'd had a home-cooked meal followed by a short nap in the long grass behind our childhood home. I take a few steps toward him, kneel in the dirt at his side. I stare at the green substance clotting the wound. It's shining *beneath* the skin, giving the flesh a dull, eerie glow, like moonlight on a pillow. I reach out to touch it. I can't help myself.

My fingertips brush his scalp, and I hear Will hiss. Not from pain, I don't think, but the *expectation* of pain.

The phosphorescent green substance is hard to define. Nothing I know equates. In some ways, it's like a clotted powder, dry, but also somehow soft, malleable. Like clay made from cloud instead of earth. I pinch a clump of it between two fingers and glowing liquid seeps out, runs down Will's temple. My fingertips tingle and a pleasant warmth rides up my hand and into my arm.

There's an open cut across my forearm, just above the wrist. I have no idea how it happened – could have been one of a thousand ways – and I frankly had not noticed it even being there. But I notice it now, because it's shining as well. Like green sunlight through a crack in a thin wall. I touch the wound on my wrist gently as the green begins to clot over the length of the cut. I smile despite myself because the skin is mending, feel the soothing of the tissue beneath, healing me.

Energized and excited despite my grim surroundings, I grab at the coat clotting William's stomach and lift it free, drop it carelessly into the dirt.

His whole stomach glows.

"Will, I'm gonna pull some of your clothes free so I can get a closer look here, alright?"

William still looks away, but he nods. I think he might be crying but it's hard to say, and I'm moving too fast to worry about it right now.

I spread his coat open wide, unbutton his shirt and pull it free from his pants. His undershirt is soaked through with blood and I grip the sides where it's been gashed and pull. It rips open like cobwebs, exposing my brother's injury.

The green powder is crusted in a six-inch crescent just below his rib cage. It's so bright I must squint my eyes to get a proper look at the damage. Like his head, I see the glow through his skin, large patches of it in his guts, chest and side. The green inside him has a slight pulse, and seems to be... swirling... spiraling inside my brother's body.

"Will," I say. "Does it hurt?"

William turns his head toward me, tears streaking clean rivulets in his dirty face. He's smiling and his eyes are bright. He looks beautiful. "It don't hurt, Henry. Honest to God, I've never felt better."

I lick my lips and press at the flesh around the wound, the green powder – *or is it liquid, like thick syrup, or molasses*

– that clings to William's skin seems to reach for me, branching toward my fingertips, climbing underneath my filthy nails. And I let it. "Any of this hurt, when I press?"

Will shakes his head, smiles like he's the cat who got the canary. "No," is all he can say, and the word comes out choked, a joyful sob.

Overhead, artillery beats like drums in the night sky. We are surrounded by corpses and fire; the stink of blood and decaying flesh fills the air. We are exhausted and emptied and sick of war, of death and the fear of death. But right now, in this moment, we laugh, and we feel exaltation course through us. I kiss my brother on the forehead and he swats me and we *laugh,* and then we cry. I cry harder than I have since I was a child, and William cries with me, laughing through snot and tears and filth. Because my brother is alive. A miracle. He's been saved. There is life among us yet.

III.

An hour passes, and I fall asleep next to my brother.

I dream of the angel that stood over William as I marched away. The mythical beast lays somewhere in the dark. It's cold there. Wet. The angel is badly injured. In the dream, I float high above the creature, like pure spirit. Spirit or not, it sees me plain. Golden, imploring eyes lock onto me. It raises, with great effort, one long, muscled arm. It points at me. I shake my head, try to pull higher, further away from its massive form, its pleading eyes. Its fingers turn into a claw, like a drowning man in a stormy sea of shadows, and I am the only one there to pull him up, help him free. But I do not.

It opens its mouth and howls. I realize that it is broken, beaten.

It bleeds.

The screams wake me, but I realize now these are human screams. The trees to the west have caught fire and men, too wounded to crawl, to save themselves, are burning alive. Despite the heavy dark of night, the moist chill of the air, everything is lit by the dancing orange flames, the heat enough to make sweat pour from my face.

"Will!" I yell, smoke clogging my nostrils. Death-cries and shell-explosions pour like poison into my ears. I shake him and he stirs. I notice the green substance that settles inside and atop his body is less than it was. Thinner, as if evaporating. But the wounds do not bleed, and the skin seems pale on his scalp and stomach. Free of infection. Healthy. "We have to move!"

I stand and shake loose dirt and leaves from my sleeves and head. I pull up the right sleeve and inspect the gash. Both it and the green matter that emblazoned it are gone. I rub at the area and feel no discomfort, no scar. The wound is healed completely.

I grab Will's arm and pull him to his feet. He winces, but no more. He's smiling again, looking down at himself, studying the rent in his clothes and flesh. "God damn," he says, and then it's my turn to wince, despite my heathen nature, my lack of belief.

"Let's make for the first camp," I say.

Although the second Union camp is closer, the odds of it staying under Confederate control are low-to-none. An unhealthy thought to have in the pitch of battle, as one wants to refrain from pessimism when in a killing skirmish, but sense is sense, and I see no reason to put us more deeply into harm's way if there is an alternative.

The luminescence of moonlight and fire assure our footing as we crest a nearby hill. Another cluster of trees burn to our left, but we stay as far from the fresh flames as we can, ignore the cries for help as they pass us by. Either distant or underfoot, it makes no difference. We are not caregivers, but survivors. We have no food or water or comfort to offer. For no reason at all I kick a man's jaw when he tugs at my cuff, begging for sustenance. We are no longer boys at play, wearing too-large coats and hunting rifles on our backs. We are dying men strolling through the hard terrain of Hell itself, and there is no such thing as mercy, for the land is burned black, and the bodies are horrific as a Bosch canvas, stretched to cover the entirety of the earth. We are pale dots, moving through demons and carnage.

At the start, I support William, his arm over my shoulders, light as a gutted fox due to my surge in strength, my refreshed constitution. Halfway to camp, I hardly notice when Will removes his arm, walks steadily beside me, one hand lightly pressed to his stomach, his cap pulled down over the luminescent tissue above his temple, where the bullet tore through his scalp. I glance at him, notice the hand seems almost protective. He doesn't seem to be holding his guts in, but rather cradling the healing power there, pulling strength from whatever it is the miraculous green substance offers.

Part of me yearns to pull his hand away from the

wound, put my own over his stomach as one might to a woman long in term, small kicks under a swollen belly. *Life!* I want to rip his coat apart, nuzzle my head there, feel the flowing strength of the panacea against my cheek. To bite it off his flesh and feel it digest. To lick it clean.

"Henry..."

I find myself staring at William's stomach. I'm drooling.

"Henry!" William repeats. He's afraid, but not of me. It's ahead of us that he looks, wide-eyed, mouth gawping, pointed hand trembling.

I follow his eyes and see we've nearly arrived at the camp. Men lay strewn haphazardly throughout, some sleeping, most wounded, many dead. There are smoldering campfires, the flames kept small and hidden so as not to draw attention from a hilltop scout giving direction to a Union battery.

There's yelling and scurrying about. Men argue. Soldiers who have never shown fear on a battlefield are now on their knees, hands clasped beneath their chins in prayer, mouths forming the words in near-silence, their eyes shut tight. There's a loud argument between two men, one in nothing but dirty white underclothes, the other swinging mercilessly at his head. They go down in a heap and there's the sick sound of bone snapping, punches connecting with meat, then pulp.

My first thought is that the battle has turned more savagely than I imagined, and these are blues invading our camp, taking it to us in hand-to-hand, sweeping us off their hill, away from their tents and charred meals.

"Look at them," William says, and I assume him to mean the skirmishes, the prayers. "Look at the bodies."

Wounded soldiers lay on the ground, or sit hunched up near small fires, formed in a ring of anticipation outside a surgeon's tent. "My god in heaven," I say, and know now why the men fight. Why the men pray.

Like William, their damaged bodies, their wounds, glisten bright and green as malachite. Hundreds of men laughing, crying. Hundreds of others gone mad with fear.

We skirt around a group of soldiers in a fierce quarrel, each of them stopping occasionally to gesture wildly at the affected soldiers. Most of the wounded and dying are shirtless, or without pants, shoes. Gunshot shoulders and stabbed chests, bullet-torn necks, missing limbs. All luminescent with the brightness of new grass on a spring day.

One man reclines against a rocky outcropping set into

the hill, his left eye vacant but for the eerie glow. His whole head seems alight, and his good eye follows us as we pass, lips curled in a knowing smile, his teeth dull white through blood-crusted beard.

The true horror are the men we find on the outskirts of the camp's eastern ridge, where more surgeon tents have been set up and where soldiers, or parts of soldiers, have been brought in the hope for care. These men are mostly dead, but even so they are *still* affected. One soldier is nothing but torso, his body ripped free from the hips down. The shredded edge of his insides glow defiantly, his wide-eyed stare into the abyss oblivious of whatever healing properties are being played out on his tissue. There are others, dead and pale, some stripped naked – by surgeons or scavengers I know not – with their various wounds bright and shining in the dark night, guiding the eye to missing limbs or gaping cuts. There is a soldier bare to the waist. His back is riddled with six clean bullet holes, perhaps grape shot. His flesh looks like a constellation, each hole a glistening star, bright green in the white space of his depleted body, his knobby spine a celestial equator.

A man's heightened cry splits the air, louder even than the constant shelling from the gunboats in the river. My blood runs cold at the sound of it, for it's the shrill desperate cry of murder. Different than when a man yells out in fear of an onrushing army, distinguished by its nakedness and surprise, its disbelief, its horror. I spin to the sound in time to see two soldiers stabbing the man into the earth with their bayonet-tipped muskets. One of these soldiers cries out "devil!" again and again. Other men with the glow begin to crawl away from the scene, on hands and knees or just elbows, panicked at the possibility of being called out next as a spawn of Satan. The cries of the murdered man cease, and the two turn their attention to the others. A pistol-shot splits the air and one of these killers goes down clutching at his chest.

In the next moment, pandemonium.

Brothers in combat, brothers in arms, now divide and come to fierce battle over the curse, the miracle of what's happening to the wounded and dead. Of what happened to William. To myself.

"William," I say, and he nods in return. His eyes are wide and white with fright. A fright I have not seen on his face – nor mine – since the start of the war.

My final image of the massacre is that of a Dixie Grey

holding a cocked pistol between the uplifted arms of the man with one green eye, and pulling the trigger.

Any men who can run do so, into the dark, away from the fight, from the slaughter. My brother and I follow without hesitation. Our goal is nothing more than to find shelter, perhaps realign with a company, be ready to take it to Grant at the break of dawn. To forget the madness within our ranks.

As we run, my thoughts are disrupted by a brilliant streak of lightning splitting the horizon in two with a jagged flash. Thunder crashes and rumbles, the pounding sound of fiery stallions the size of planets racing before Elijah's chariot across the heavens, and the swelled clouds burst apart from the concussion of it and a resurgent, torrential rain crashes down.

APRIL 7, 1862

The Second Day

I.
After leaving the brutal scene at the camp, we run away from the worst of the battle, away from the murders.

The land is full of tough thickets of arching angel oaks, tight groups of slash pine, sunken ravines and knee-deep swamp. Hell of a place to fight a war, as one can barely walk a straight line, much less run when shot upon. I suppose the terrain forces a man to turn and fight, and maybe that's what the gods want.

Will and I run to cover among the trees, thinking we'll find shelter from the driving, constant rain, as if the trees for a hundred yards in every direction aren't ripped apart by artillery and bullets, or burned to charcoal stumps. We see more men out here. Dead men, already bloating, swarmed by flies. A few are still alive, moaning and crying out for water, food, home. Yankees and Confederates both. Some lay twined together, forever holding the pose of deadly battle. There are pieces of men: An arm stuck into the crook of a split trunk, a hooked leg stemming from a growing puddle of rainwater, or, in places, nothing but a squelch of red meat to step into by accident, like you might a slick of dark mud.

But it isn't until we see the men in the thicket, these goddamned *glowing* men, that we lose what remains of our minds. At first we only study them, quietly, neither of us saying two words to rub together.

We don't think to eat the dead ones. Not at first.

It's only when we see the first living soldier, wheezing with his head bent against a tree, neck broken and glowing like a bright moon, that the idea generates.

William falls to his knees and I watch, solemn and silent. Curious. He puts a hand on the man's head, mumbles something I can't hear over the rain. The man may be healing but so far his neck still looks broken, his breathing labored, his limbs still, lifeless. Will lowers his head to the soldier's own, as if to kiss him goodnight. He puts his mouth on the back of that neck, the skin pointedly bulged where a bone pushes out, and starts to lick at it. Lots of the green lies under the skin, but enough on top, as well. Will's fervor grows. He begins to gnaw at the green crust, pull it off the skin with his teeth, swallow it down. He sounds like a man sucking soup from a ladle, like a dog cleaning a dish. The soldier with the bent neck starts to weep, but I don't think Will hears.

A faint glow a few yards off. I walk over. It's a boy. An Aide. Must have been. Doubt he ever saw fourteen years. Probably a musician, or a messenger. Somebody's son or younger brother. That might well have been his father nearby, broken against the tree. The one William works on. The boy has been well split by artillery. There is only one leg in the dirt, the other lost in the wet dark.

He has green all over him. Crusted over half his face, a hand, the stump of a thigh. I try to be sensitive, at first using my fingers to wipe the stuff free before putting it between my lips; but, like Will, something comes over me, something sweet and musical. Like sliding into a warm bath, or a warm woman. My God, its divine! I'm trembling as I put my mouth on him and feel myself stiffen. My mind roars between my ears as I close my eyes and let the ecstasy push through my skin, fry my every nerve.

I do my best to take my time with him, and leave little.

Through the heavy rain, the pungent smells of charred wood and meat fill the air, and we go on. Body to body. If they are healed enough to fight we cut their throats, then wait and watch. Tiny insects flock to the fresh wounds. We watch in stunned awe as the new cuts fill with the luminescent green. The miracle emerges from nothing to form thick liquid which bubbles a little, then hardens, scabs over. We wait as long as we are able during this transformation, and often leave to find others, then come back to the more recently killed. Part of me wants to study the morality of our action, but unlike those in the camp, our dealing is merciful. There is no anger, no bloodlust.

There is only the need.

I find myself watching Will out of one eye as I explore other options, make sure he isn't returning to the newly-opened before I do, as we had agreed to entreat upon these together. I trust my brother, but in a room full of gold even the most trustworthy have sly pockets and silver tongues.

I shake off these dark thoughts. There is more than enough. The battle has seen to that – yes, oh yes. It is truly a garden of delights. A perfect Eden. After the first few bodies are picked clean, the thicket no longer seems burnt and shattered, but instead I see a light-filled orchard dense with ripe fruit. Golden apples fallen from trees, shining in tall soft grass that is soft as feathers on our chins when we bend low. It is a wonderland, a dream world. The thunder and constant barrage of artillery from the gunboats are as rhythmic as ocean waves, the pre-dawn sky a shower of swirling silver-dust stars, the moon a pale-faced mother, whispering the secrets of life with cratered lips.

After a few hours, neither one of us can take in anymore. My mind is bursting with the most beautiful colors; my body sings and tingles. My full stomach, a tight ball beneath my belt, gives off a warmth and comfort I cannot get enough of.

It seems that no matter how full we are, there is always room for more.

There is an epiphanous state we can *almost* reach, *almost* feel. If we can only, somehow, absorb more of the viridity that surrounds us, that grows like sponge pudding on the torn flesh of a body the way cream curdles into butter when stamped inside a churn, then perhaps we could surmount that ledge, blossom like wildflowers in a field of light, extend our petals wide – bright and alive – and fill ourselves with honey sunshine until we burst open, spilling golden dust to catch warm wind, shooting higher... higher...

We are sitting, heel-to-heel, when William has the idea.

I hesitate, but am admittedly fascinated by the possibilities.

It is William who cuts himself first.

II.

The sky is smeared charcoal. The occasional pinprick of starlight slips through the heavy smoke ceiling of the day's battle, the arsenal continuing, without cease, from the gunships. The occasional answer of our cannon sounds weak and irritated in comparison. I wonder if Grant's supposition is that he'll drive us all mad with the noise, leaving nothing but idiots to fight in the oncoming dawn.

"I need more, Henry," William says.

I notice the tremble in his voice. The *need*. I know it's there because it's in me as well. Desperate and hungry and unyielding. I truly empathize. "Okay," I say, not knowing what else to offer, thinking he means to hunt a different patch of land for more bodies. It wouldn't be difficult; the green glow is visible enough against the draped night that a walk of a hundred yards would likely bring more carrion.

I start to stand but he catches my arm. "No, not that."

He reaches fast and slips the bowie knife from my boot, and for a wild second I think he is readying to plunge it into my chest. I draw back with sucked breath, hands up to defend myself.

He laughs. "Easy, big brother," he says.

For a moment, it's as if my eyes truly open. In that laugh, the people we used to be rises to the forefront of my mind, bobbing on the surface of the great black lake of my consciousness. The need is forgotten, only for a moment, as I recall the boys we were only months before. The fine estate that our mother and father inherited from our grandfather, a tobacco farmer with two hundred acres. Our beautiful little sister, entering the dining room with the newest fashion, readying herself for the season. Our mother kissing us goodnight when we were children. Will and I sharing a room with a house full of them, because we were so desperate for each other's company. I used to think we shared dreams. Part of me wonders about that now, as Will slides the sharp point of my knife up the length of one bare arm, blood shining like a trickle of oil in the smoke-curtained moonlight. I wonder if this is a dream. I know, deep in my heart, that it very well could be. Or perhaps we are dead, or dying. Lying bent and broken in a swamp, down the slope of a ravine, or in the thick brambles of a forest's skirt. Could this be us playing out our lives in an ethereal state? A purgatory?

I nod as I watch his bloodied arm, waiting. Hoping. I agree with the premise, firmed by the demons I've seen on the field this day, the angel watching over my brother as I ran off to a fresh skirmish. Yes, a death dream. The feeling only swells more true within me as I watch William's arm begin to hum with that familiar viridescent radiance. It starts beneath the skin, and Will sighs in a sort of ecstasy. I watch, fascinated, as the same tiny insects swarm over him. Black, microbic things. Like fleas. They buzz and crawl in and out of the bloody ruin... before my very eyes it crystalizes. I smell the sharp tang of urine and see William has relieved himself, his crotch staining, a slow trickle dripping from the cuff of a pant leg.

"Henry," he says. "it's like heaven is inside me." He laughs. "It's so sweet, brother."

He hands me back the knife and I study it a moment before taking it. Part of me is afraid. The idea of self-mutilation, even to achieve such a glorious state, frightens me. Both physically and, I suppose, spiritually. There is a wrongness to it that I struggle with, and the irony is not lost on me that I've likely killed, and murdered, easily twenty men in the last day, but the feeling is there regardless.

"Go on," he says. "Then I want another turn."

I nod and pull free of my jacket. I roll up my sleeve, stare at the soft white flesh of my arm. I cut it open, wrist-to-elbow, and cry out despite myself at the fiery pain that spikes into my body. I wait for the sting to become a throb. When it does, I stare transfixed at my wound.

I watch it fill, as it did with William. I worried it might not work on me, so did not cut deep. But as that warmth begins to seep into my arm, the streaming rivers of my veins, my brain, I wish I'd pushed in deeper. More savagely. The desire is so strong it takes all of me to keep the knife at my side, to enjoy the wash of love and comfort that drowns me.

"It looks like emeralds," he says vacantly, close enough to sniff the skin. I hadn't seen him move so close. I push him away, but do not disagree.

Will goes for his belly next. Near his former wound, which is now vanished as if it never was. In turn, I cut across my chest.

He asks me repeatedly, and then heatedly, to stab him with the knife, on his back and legs, to puncture him deep so the jade medicine will be sunken within him, spreading outward like a seed that sprouts green-tentacled arms and legs of vegetation, of new life. I refuse, alarmed at the veracity of his request, and I physically restrain him from doing any more harm to himself. He's losing so much blood that I worry the healing will not keep pace, and I tell him so.

"We've seen dead men with more fragile cuts than these," I say, crying out in the dark, shaky with anxiety and ecstasy.

He finally agrees, although he pouts and, I think, schemes. Perhaps waiting for me to slip into sleep, or to be gone altogether by a stray 12-pounder from one of those constantly barking gunships, leaving the field to himself alone.

III.

The world lightens, though the sun still hides beneath the scar of horizon. I had fallen asleep, and wake with a start, surprised to see the sky a deep blue with a shy pink skirt, rather than black. The rain has thankfully stopped once again. Next to me, William sleeps, content and well-nourished.

I stand, walk ten paces, and shit in the mud. I use a dead man's hat to clean myself. I scavenge further, retrieve two high-quality muskets, additional ball and powder. A second blade, which I keep, tucked into the back, held fast by my belt.

I wake William, hand him the rifle, ammunition. He accepts wordlessly and we leave the wood.

The field that separates us from the bulk of the armies is dense with corpses – man and horse. In the distance, bugle cries float through the air. I think them a call for the Union, but can't say why. The first gunshots pepper the morning, and I walk toward them with the desperate need for battle, to prove myself. We are not cowards; we're not raised to be such and would not be today. I don't turn but know William is following me, likely studying corpses, waiting on the sun.

Pounding hooves approach from the west, and a group of six cavalry ride over the bump of a blackened hill. As I watch, they pivot, head straight for me and my twin brother. Likely thinking us deserters.

A lieutenant is at their head and the first to reach us. He scowls from atop his horse. His sabre rattles at his side and he grips the butt of a pistol. Two other men in his command hold shotguns, the barrels tucked in the crooks of their arms. The others scan the field, possibly searching for more lost souls. I stand at attention, look the lieutenant in the eye. Forrest's men are not to be trifled with.

"Whose command are you?" the lieutenant says flatly, the smooth face beneath his hat having not yet seen thirty years, and likely never will.

"15th Infantry, sir. Under Smith, who I believe is dead, and Russell, who is missing." I turn my shoulder to show the acorn patch. William stands motionless and silent. "Most recently," I say, "my brother and I fought with Wood's brigade against a group of Regulars, took the sunken road over yonder. My brother was injured and our company decimated, sir. We went back to the first taken camp to regroup and see my brother's wounds cared for, and were just now heading back to the front, try and join the men in the final push."

"Your brother looks fine to me, though his uniform is a disgrace."

"Thank you, sir," is all I say, no other defense coming to mind.

The lieutenant nods, his scowl replaced with a grimace. He looks toward the Tennessee, the opening sounds of battle. "Well, it's been hell. Ruggle's battery tore most of those blues up, and their reinforcements are a day away at best. You boys make your way up, find General Polk's regiment near Water Oaks Pond, straight through there. He'll need fresh legs. Beauregard's launching a counterattack, and that should put an end to things. The Yankees are at the end of their rope. Those are your orders, men."

He starts away, but I cry out after him. "Lieutenant," I say, and he slows, turns. "There was some dark business at the camp, sir."

He looks off in the direction of the first camp, then back at me and Will. "All the business here is dark, soldier. Double-quick, now." He nods once more as if it is settled, and rides off in a storm, the handful of horse-backed men gallop in flanks behind him, toward the new day of battle. Toward victory.

"Think they'll take the landing?" William asks, and spits.

"I don't know, brother. Let's get on up there and find out what's what."

We continue walking and eventually fall in with a ragtag company half-heartedly humming *Tramp! Tramp! Tramp!* as they stomp through wet grass, the leftovers of a regiment that was overrun. Many captured, many dead. They had orders to form up with Breckinridge for the counterattack.

As we fall into the step with these Dixies, the sun breaks from the horizon, ignites the day. I see the men I'm with more clearly now, and am disheartened at their lack of strength and will. I must force myself to slow my pace, so energized and refreshed am I compared to these tired soldiers. William even more so, I believe, as he is practically at a jog beside me, his hands twitching as if desirous for more killing. I notice some of the men watch us, and wonder if they are skeptical of our fitness, if they can see us for the murderous cannibals that we are. I study William closely, looking for outward signs. His skin, I note, seems pink and warm. His eyes, when they find mine, are blazing and blackened by enlarged pupils. If not for the grime and blood caked onto his uniform I might have thought him just arrived by ferryboat, fresh from the plantation.

We climb a gentle acclivity and, once crested, see the field of battle open beneath us. The first thing I notice is the countless number of blues. Three, I think, for every one of ours. The entire company stops, flat-footed, as a battalion in the distance is overrun completely by a surge of Yankees from the north.

"My God," someone says.

"Buell, it must be Buell," comes another.

"Not possible. Beauregard would know!"

"He's pushing us into the mill, brothers. We must retreat."

Before any consensus can be made, we hear a roar of triumph from the northeast, and a thousand Confederate men – near a full regiment – rise from a dip in the land like a grey sunrise cresting the horizon, straight for us. A captain on horseback rides our way. He pulls up to our company and speaks with great animation to a 1st lieutenant down the line. They argue, and then the captain shakes his head, ending the debate, and raises his voice to command us all.

"We're falling back to Corinth Road, where we will regroup and launch a second counter-offensive. You men are with us now."

It's barely late morning, and it feels as though the battle – so fiercely fought and with such great sacrifice, a battle seemingly all but won hours earlier – is now lost.

As we march, I study the skirmish to the north. Great pillars of smoke rise from the earth, reach for the sky. Word comes from a scout that Bragg has been pushed back, and will smother the enemy along the Hamburg-Purdy Road, just north of our destination – a small white church where we first bivouacked less than two days prior. Polk's regiment is apparently close behind, and we are ordered to make haste.

Massive battery cannon is blooming, showering us with dirt as its shells strike at the land over which we'd only recently marched. The other men are tired-through, worn-thin and hungry. Two men collapse on the road and we leave them, feeling as though we are running to save our lives, the blues breathing down our backs.

We reach the church at noon, and I feel a surge of pride at the endless line of Confederates lining the Hamburg-Purdy, the seemingly endless reinforcements camped around the church, humped caissons stamping the ridge to the south, strong bunches of cavalry at the end of the line toward the western end, the massive battery – the 5th artillery – holding in place, cannon ready to hurl canister and case at the first sign of the enemy from the north. The Yankees marching south will need to traverse a great pond, which will cause delay for any batteries supporting their infantry. It will be steel versus lead, and I salivate with the desire to do battle once more. Hope riddles my brain and my body, and whether it comes from the mysterious elixir or the sight of all these great Southern men, I am fit and ready to fight. I slap William on the back and he grins at me. I know he feels the same.

A bugle bleats and a horde of blues pour over the ridge. Thousands of them.

The battery comes alive, blasting shot into the first line. Bodies splinter apart and are sent airborn. Some disintegrate completely in a shower of red.

"Don't let them breathe!" someone screams, and the muskets open. The sky is nothing but explosions and concussions of sound so great the ear could not possibly take it all in. William and I fire from a line east of the church. I prime the pan and ram the new load down when a flicker of blue to my right turns my head.

Running in pace with an entire fresh regiment of Federals, like a flooding river over a low bank, demons come pouring in force, mouths twisted, jaws snapping, white eyes brilliant hollows. Their speed is that of a flood one cannot escape.

The howls of their victory are not heard, hidden beneath the sounds of begging men, rent metal and the clashing cacophony of musket and cannon fire.

"From the east!" I scream. An explosion wipes ten men off the earth beside me, and suddenly all is chaos.

IV.

I run.

Push through bodies and curses and cries of hate, fear and pain. Through the red haze until I find William. His arm is broken and his left hand a charred stub with black ribbons, only a thumb remains. His clothes are tattered, the flesh of thigh and hip visible through burned rags of uniform. He lies on the ground babbling, his good hand clutching at the churned earth. I'm unsure if he's crawling for safety or praying for death. A demon straddles his hip and I kick at it. The thing hisses at me but skitters away into the smoke, disappears.

I lift my brother from the dirt, ignore his hot, foul scream of pain in my ear. There is only one direction to go. South. Away from the devils and the blues. Away from the Union and the war.

Home, I think. *We'll go home.*

A lieutenant approaches, an apparition in the vaporous scene, and points a finger into my face. "Back in line, scoundrel!" he barks. With my free hand I swing up my bowie knife and ram it into the soft under his chin with such force that his feet leave the ground. The power running through me has pushed the blade clean through tongue, brain and skull, only the hilt still visible. For a moment, I have the idea that I see the steel behind his eyes, the tip punching through his pate. I slide it free and he drops like a sack to the dust.

"We must flee, brother," I say, not knowing if Will can hear me, can make sense of my words. There is so much noise. Mountains punched apart by the hands of an angry and almighty God would not fill the air more completely.

The only thought is of escape, of running as far from this massacre of men as I can, of getting William to safety. My vision blurs and I realize I'm crying, and try to force myself to stop. I wipe tears from my cheekbones, the running snot from my nose. I mumble as I pull us away from the conflict, not thinking of how we'll get there, of whether we'll survive such a journey. All I know, all I can think, is *Away! Away!*

"Home, William... we must go home and get you well. Mother will to see to it. She'll see you back to health. Just hang on, dear brother, hang on..."

We pass through the supply line and the makeshift medical areas. How many dead men can I see and keep sane? How many bodies can a man watch torn to pieces, blasted to pulp, before his mind gives in and sinks into the abyss of madness? I turn away from the crowd of men who sit or lay, waiting to be healed as more are dragged and dropped, a continuous flow of death.

A horse free of rider shoots from the mist. It froths at

the mouth. Musket flashes dance in its wide, black eyes. It knocks us down and tramples onward, seeking that abyss, or perhaps already, in its mind, riding through it, running, running through blackness, desperate for the light. Any light.

I get to my knees and turn back only once, the irrational fear pinging my brain that I'll be turned to salt in the process, but cannot help myself. I see the steeple of the small church in the distance. It's being licked clean by fire.

William is unmoving but I hoist him up, carry him forward. My beautiful burden.

The first camp lies ahead (the second now long overrun, the dead campfires and befouled tents taken back by the Union), and we make for it. There is a mass of soldiers gathered there. One shoots another and they scatter. I don't know what is left to argue for among us. The spoils of defeat? The looting of the scrapheap? Still, I hesitate. I want no more of bloodshed, and am concerned the place might be a killing ground for the retreating, the lost. Soon enough the entire army would fall back, whatever is left of us, and order will be restored. But now, at this place, it is only desperation and madness. I decide to move off Corinth Road, make my way through the bramble and ravines. Better to fight the rough land and survive than to take the well-trod road and be gutted.

Someone yells out and I somehow *know* it is intended for us. Without pause, I break clean off the road, push myself harder than I ever have, my gimping twin at my side, whimpering and affixed to my hip as if we were born connected that way, bound by flesh as well as spirit. I smile ruefully and blink back more tears, swallow the emotion. The heartache of a life passed by, the loss of a childhood, of innocence. We are dogs now, filthy and murderous, but we were *good* men. Proud Southern men. The emptiness is so total as to almost capsize me, and I let out a moan as I run, men calling for me to turn back, the dead trees ahead reaching out to welcome me in, to the wilderness, to some wizened, glorious death.

"Don't leave me, Will," the tear-choked words spill from me as I push for the trees. "Please don't leave me alone out here."

We enter the trees and, as far as the cold world will ever know, we disappear.

V.

A gash in the earth. A deep ravine I know we must circumvent. All the trees here are burned, and small flames still tickle black wood in a few of the dead trunks. The upper stratum that ridges the ravine is warm and covered in ash. I peer over the edge to gauge the depth. I yelp as flaked rock crumbles beneath my feet and suddenly I'm sliding, pulling the all-but-lifeless body of my brother down with me.

I flip and catch something jagged in my back. I spin in the air, cry out with pain before a stout boulder smacks into my jaw, cracking something deep. I lose strength in my limbs and my ears fill with a high-pitched ween. I crash into the bottom of the ravine, a stream puddling over smooth stones fills my mouth and nostrils. Somehow, I'm able to turn my face away, let the icy water soak my back and boots. I try to take deep breaths – unsure as to the degree of the damage done to me – when it comes:

William!

I force myself to a sitting position, my head spinning, vision blurred. I vomit into the water. I feel a hard click in my jawline and give a muffled groan. I try to call out for William but my mouth only hangs open, bent and broken, the nerves either paralyzed or severed.

William's body is downstream, ten yards away. He is face-down but clear of the water. He shows no signs of being alive.

It's then I notice the colors of the water. Green tendrils run through the thin, shallow stream, like frayed strings with no beginning or end. The sight fills me with uncertain hope, and I make it to my knees. After a few deep breaths, I don't feel the nausea, but I know the damage in my face is severe, and my back burns with a deep puncture. I slowly raise my eyes, study my new surroundings.

It is a deep hollow, and I track the descent from the ridge to be twenty feet. The sides are bramble and boulder, the odd stark tree. The one nearest me is tilted, its pale, dirt-smeared roots bared on the downslope, crawling toward the stream like long wicked fingers.

The stream itself travels to the north, the source of it past the prone body of my brother, another good ten yards. At a point, it bends to the left and into a cleft cut into a wall of brittle shale, pale as exposed bone. I crawl in that direction to reach William. I can't tell if he's breathing, and roll him over onto his back.

He does breathe. His eyes peel open and find me.

I try to speak, but my jaw is slack and unmoving. I point to the opening, a dark mouth from which the stream trickles, infused with the green luminescence we've seen on the field of battle. His head turns listlessly to the side, following my indication, then back to me.

"Water," he rasps, and I wonder if he knows what it is he asks for, if he is aware of what it contains. I wonder further why the damned thought hadn't yet entered my bruised brain.

The water.

For now, I ignore his plea and sink my own face into the stream. I slurp as best able, and taste the sweetness mingled with the cold. Within seconds my mind clears, as if a frail cotton veil has been lifted free by the medicine, torn away by a gust of heavenly wind.

Feeling recuperated, I tend to William. I pull him by the collar toward the stream, turn him over so his face lies at the edge of its apron. His tongue slides out and the water passes over it. His throat works to swallow whatever meager drops enter his mouth. After a few moments, he's turned himself over completely, elbows dug into stones, gulping the water hungrily in great swallows.

As for me, my eyes stray continuously to the jagged split in the earth from which the stream emanates, and I know I must go inside and see the source of all this magic. I stand, swaying. My head is clear but throbbing with a dull pain. My back is torn, but I can already feel the green fluid coursing to the wound, slowing the blood and warming my insides.

I walk toward the opening, see the virescent fluid concentrating, flowing out of the gap like sap from a tapped tree, like thick blood from an opened vein. William is behind me, standing on his own power now. I do not turn to look at him. The thought of seeing half his charred body coated in the luminescent moss would be too much to bear, and I fear my envy would force me to evil discourse.

I duck into the gap, and the air grows chill and moist. The tunnel is narrow and dark. It slopes slowly downward, and after only a few minutes of walking I finally turn, look back, past my brother's looming shadow to the slit of sky beyond, already minimized to a broken blue finger in an expanse of black.

"Henry, keep going for God's sake," Will says, his voice

a rusted command, the remnants of his lost hand already pulsing with a fervid green glow.

I nod and turn back to the dark, feeling my way deeper into the earth. Fingers tremble over slick rock walls, feet step lightly forward and down, forward and down.

A hundred steps and now all is complete dark. There is no slice of daylight behind, no darker shade of blackness ahead to guide our direction. A gust of stale air slides over me, and far off – deep, deep down – a pulse of dull jade. My heart quickens and I stumble forward faster, faster, nearly tripping to my knees but catching my balance, propelling myself into the bowels of this place, this open vein of mother earth.

As we near the source of the light, more wisps of air drift against my face, as if there is an open window ahead, the evening's breeze passing through, a delicate intruder. Quite suddenly, the path tilts, straightens, and expands. Flat now, and wider, we no longer temper our strides. An opening looms, and beyond it a light, brilliant after so much darkness, that comes from the very walls of what appears as a chamber, a great cavernous heart in the chest of this body of rock and earth, that we have entered. Invaded.

I stumble through the breach and see the heart's inner workings.

"Oh God!" I cry, and drop to my knees.

Will leaps past me, screaming something I cannot understand, perhaps simply ranting, or singing. His mind must have snapped, for he is turning in circles, now jumping, throwing himself at the very walls. Past him is spread the epicenter of this veined, throbbing organ. The means of all this end.

The angel.

It lies atop a massive slab of stone. Its spear lies bloodied and useless on the ground beside it. The thick flesh of the thing has been ripped and torn at every inch, decimated by claws and teeth. On the hard floor surrounding the altar is an impossible pool of blood, the color brilliant as torchlight, gold and sparkling swirled together with a glaucous dust. I step closer to it, my own wounds forgotten in the wonder of this fallen creature. Closer now, I see its flesh has been torn cleanly from bone in places, and clumps of pulpy, dark red muscle lie dormant on the stone.

Studying the wounds, I envisage the great fight it must have waged against a horde of the demons. A vision blooms in my imagination, and I see blinding light come from its palms, throwing them back. But it is not enough. I watch the spear, swinging and stabbing in great sweeps that would topple a hundred men, as it shreds the smoky flesh of the devils.

But still they came, didn't they angel?

Yes, they came. Until you were overwhelmed, and they swarmed over you, shredding your earth-bound meat and sinew, ripped your hair free in clumps, tore and gnashed at your flesh with needle-prick teeth. And still you fought until finally – with nothing left – you killed the last of them, the rest fleeing, finding other battles to wage. You could not save the men on the field, because Hell's armies are countless. They are multitudes. They are legion, and you are just one soldier. One sacrifice.

Then, spent and dying, you crawled your way here. To sanctuary. To a final communion with your distant God. And here you bleed, and the earth greedily soaks in your substance, absorbs the holy architecture of your molecules, of your life's breath.

The vision recedes, my eyelids flicker, as if just now fully awake.

In the area around the body are rivulets that extend from the pool of blood. The fluid turns from gold to green when amalgamated with the earth's minerals. The tiny rivers flow like a spider web in every direction, toward the cavern walls, where the green veins have crept upward, like ivy, into the rich soil, to infest the meat of the earth, to engorge the worms and the insects.

The men.

A cathedral of such holy measure has never been made on this planet. Such a living testament to God's seed never suffused so fully into mankind.

I think of my father, of how he would have given away his very soul to be standing where I stand, see the remains of the fallen angel's body, laid out as a sacrifice to the mortals, its blood fueling the earth and the dying soldiers in kind. What the savior did in allegory, so this creature does in raw truth.

My brain reaches for other parallels – the giving of life, the sacrifice – but I cannot. For it *lives*. Its eyes fix on mine. There is no anger, no discord. Only sympathy. A weary sadness that shakes me.

I drop to my knees by the golden pool, splay my fingers and rest my palms on its surface. It is a wild, boundless ecstasy.

Elation surges through me like an exploding star. I spasm and gasp at the strength of it.

As I relish this feeling, a shadow passes by me. I have barely thought enough left to notice this other, so rapt am I with the gift of transformation. My vision is spiraling, and all is cast with the tint of a golden glow, the dark as bright now as the day. The hairs on my scalp and body crinkle, as if from intense heat, and fall away.

William is climbing atop the altar. His head nestles deep into the waist of the creature, where he suckles like a newborn.

The creature's face never turns, never alters. Its eyes still bore into me. Such great sorrow! I stand slowly, as if in a trance, and look about the chamber for my need. I reach for one that will do the work and pick it up, feel the elements coursing inside of it. The age of it.

I slip my knife free with the other hand, and step through the pool of golden blood.

I plunge the blade deep into my brother's back. He squawks but only grabs more firmly to the rich meat. With a great effort – my strength not only renewed but ten-fold – I pull on the exposed hilt and drag my twin free of his feast. He drops from the stone, spasms and splashes in the pool in some wild bliss. I leave the knife and grab his wrist, drag him across the rocky floor, away from the healing blood. I drop him onto his chest. He tries to turn, to fight, but my weight falls on the knife handle, driving the blade straight through, pinning him as his limbs gyrate and his body trembles.

"Henry!" he shouts – a question or a plea I know not. I bring down the heavy, jagged stone onto his skull.

My memories – those of my mother, of my family, of my home – blow free of my mind like dust as I lift the stone and drop it once more. I do this again and again, until he is past the point of any miraculous redemption.

My breath coming in heaves, I fall away. I leave his flesh as it is, stuck and bludgeoned. Seeing his crushed face is like seeing myself laying there. As if moving on without my body, I turn away, crawl back toward the golden pool, the sacrifice.

I bring my lips to the aureate slick, and I drink.

After a while, after it is enough, I stand. My body is longer than it was. There is a reshaping of muscles and bone inside me, a painful but necessary reinvention. There are stones in my mouth and I spit them out. My sight expands; my vision takes in every direction at a single glance. Like frail tissue I pull the clothes from my body, look down at the heap of them, see eyes and teeth settled into the crevices of the dark stone floor.

My lengthened arms, black and slick, reach for the great creature, and a long tongue works its way into my mouth, the forked tip pushes into my cheek.

I stand beside the angel, look down with newfound knowledge... and consuming fear. Its haunted eyes are no longer sorrowful, but alive with command. I lay a hand upon its chest, and move to nuzzle its chin and neck, to find the veins there and open them.

Its eyes halt me, if only for a moment.

"What am I?" I say, but do not recognize the words, the shape of them; or the sound. Foreign, yet familiar. "What am I *now*?"

"Bound," the angel says softly, its words dried leaves in an August breeze, and closes its great eyes in submission. "Eternally bound to this abyss. This dank purgatory. To the shadows, and to the great evil that lies in the dark."

A moan, thick with regret, escapes me.

With it my humanity.

I dip my head to drink, forever damned.

SODA JERK
A Sabbath Story

Carrie-Ann looked down from her bedroom window and watched the yellow moving van pull out of their new driveway, into the street, and disappear behind a large shaggy tree that craned upward from their front yard toward blue so bright and clear that the clouds were nothing more than bursts from far-off cannons, small puffs of smoke crawling along the surface. The sky was so perfect it seemed creation itself was smiling down on her – her new home, her new life. She looked into that vast blue and wanted to smile back, feel the joy it offered, but found she could not. Perhaps it was too blue, she thought. Too expansive, too true. The sky was a lie, after all, a shiny trapdoor that hid the whole universe behind its fragile, curved shell. She drew a humped line on the thin glass of the window to match the shape of her mouth, brushed her fingers along the lace curtains hung prior to her arrival, and turned away.

She sat down heavily on the bare mattress of her bed and stared at the neat stacks of boxes that held all her worldly goods. She eyeballed the furniture placed haphazardly around the room, moved them piece-by-piece in her mind to different parts of the space. Nothing seemed to fit just right, and a knot of frustration tightened inside her. She smoothed her cotton dress over her knees, calming herself. She studied the tips of her white sneakers while fighting back a swell of tears. *A sixteen-year-old girl should not have to start over*, she thought. She'd spent the last ten years building her *life*. Now that life might as well be a million miles away, on a distant planet for all the good it did her. She had loved Chicago, her school, her girlfriends, her old room...

All gone. Swept away like dust.

"Carrie-Ann Miles, you are the unluckiest girl in the whole, wide world," she said, the words drifting to the floor like dead autumn leaves.

Downstairs, someone knocked at the front door.

Momentarily distracted from her self-pity, she ran back to the window and looked down, expecting to see a wide-assed neighbor holding a Bundt cake, or the local pastor, bible under one elbow, ready to welcome new sheep to his venerated flock. She put her palms to the frame, lifted her heels to stand on tiptoes, strained to see who would visit them on the very day, near the very *hour*, of their arrival. She saw a sun-kissed, shimmering cherry-red Chrysler ragtop in the driveway, but the jutted roof blocked her view of the porch and the stranger on the porch. She ran to her bedroom door, pushed her ear against it and listened as her mother crossed the floor to answer. Her clipped, subterranean steps echoed off the walls of the starkly-furnished home.

The front door opened and she heard excited voices. A young man's voice by the sound, and her mother's high-pitched fake laugh, the one she used at cocktail parties and while on the phone with old friends. Carrie-Ann moved deftly to the top of the stairs, looked down at slanted squares of bare white walls and polished wood floors. She peered over the railing, saw the back of her mother's calves and a pair of black sneakers pointed forward, then moving.

The door closed and Carrie-Ann pulled away from the railing, out of sight, inexplicably held her breath.

"Carrie-Ann!" her mother called, her voice bouncing off the bare floors and walls.

"Yes?" she replied flatly, her porcelain-skinned hands resting on the bannister, her chin lifted regally in anticipation of being introduced.

"Can you come down please?"

As no faces appeared beneath her to look up and notice her perfect positioning, Carrie-Ann blew out a breath and walked down the stairs, stopping just short of the bottom to maintain superiority of height.

She saw the lithe frame of her mother, dolled up in a white dress with light pink polka-dots, her blond hair pulled back from porcelain features. Beside her stood a tall, skinny boy. He smiled down at her mother with stunning white teeth; his high, tanned cheek-bones shining like polished brass. He had a bold pompadour of slicked black hair, glistening like a black ocean atop a broad forehead.

Carrie-Ann coughed lightly, announcing herself. She felt color rise to her cheeks when the boy's eyes met hers. They were of the brightest blue, piercingly so, like the sky above her new town. Blue eyes were her favorite.

"How do you do?" she asked politely, staying on the stairs for now.

"Honey..." her mother started, as if to reprimand, then brightened. "Carrie-Ann, this is James. James... what was your last name, dear?"

"Honeycutt."

"Of course," she said, giggling as if he'd goosed her behind. "Honeycutt. James Honeycutt. James has come to welcome us to the neighborhood. Come here and say hello. He won't bite, will you James?"

"No mam," he said, those white teeth shining.

Carrie-Ann went to them slowly, lifted a hand and allowed James to shake it.

"James goes to your new high school. He's the class president, isn't that something?" her mother said, all but scribbling out wedding announcements in her head while she did so.

"That's true," James said humbly, "and as such it's my job to come meet any new students, show them around, make them feel welcome."

Carrie-Ann nodded. Even she was taken off-guard by the boy's sincerity and obvious kindness. And he was such a strong, handsome, obviously popular boy; traits she rarely found in combination with generosity of spirit, at least with the boys back home.

"I see," was all she said in response.

"I gather you have a lot of unpacking to do, but perhaps, when you're settled, you'd allow me to escort you around our fine town, show you some highlights, introduce you to some of the locals."

"Oh, well, there is a lot yet to do..."

"That is the most wonderful thing I've ever heard of!" her mother interjected, giving Carrie-Ann a cunning look. "You two should do exactly that. James, dear, what are your plans today?"

"As it happens," James said, "I'm quite free. I was going to offer to take Carrie-Ann this afternoon, but then I saw how much work there is to be done here... hey, I'd be glad to stay and help move some things around."

"Nonsense!" her mother said so loudly Carrie-Ann jumped in her skin. "Harry, that's my husband, will be home from his new job in just a few hours and he and I will get everything in its place. You two kids should go and have fun, really. Carrie-Ann, you should take a sweater in case the night gets chilly."

Night? she thought, hesitating.

"Go on, dear," her mother said, in a polite yet firm tone that was not to be denied. "Go get your blue sweater. I hung it in your closet with a few dresses so you'd have something to wear until we got settled. Go on, hurry up, James doesn't have all day."

"Oh, no hurry at all, it would be my pleasure," James said silkily, and smiled at her, those blue eyes twinkling like ice on a sunny day. "I have a few things I think you'll be real interested to see."

"So," she said, warm under the glass of the wide windshield, but not wanting to put her window down for fear of mussing her hair, "how long have you lived in Sabbath?"

"All my life, of course," he said, steering the massive red car out of the suburban street and onto Lakeview Drive, the town's one main road that circumnavigated the lake it surrounded. She felt the power of the car beneath her as he sped up, the purr of the engine belying its unleashed force.

"Why 'of course'," she said, trying to subtly catch her face in the side mirror to check her lips.

"Oh, I guess I just mean, you know, why live anywhere else? As far as I'm concerned, Sabbath is the most wonderful place on God's green earth."

Carrie-Ann laughed, not able to help herself. "And how would you know that, James Honeycutt? Have you been everywhere else on earth?"

He turned and smiled at her, as if playing along, but his blue eyes weren't twinkling like they had been. They looked hard and flat, like dead sky. She made a point to not break eye-contact with him, despite his steely gaze, and she wondered if this boy, no more than a year or two her senior, perhaps *had* been all over the world. There was knowledge in those eyes.

"Jimmy," he said, his gaze softening.

"Sorry?"

He looked toward the road once more. "Call me Jimmy. All my pals do."

Pals, eh? That'd be a first for me, she thought. *The boys back home certainly never wanted to be "pals."*

"Thanks," she said shortly, making sure not to sound impressed. "So, Jimmy, where are we headed on our whirlwind tour of the wondrous, God-given, eighth wonder of the world that is the town of Sabbath?" She laughed a little so he wouldn't think her bitchy, and he smiled along this time.

"First stop is the lake. It's the heart and soul of our little town, so it makes sense we introduce you first thing."

"Well, I'll be sure to be on my best behavior," she said, pleased to have a new boy to flirt with.

"That'd be wise," he responded tonelessly, and her smile vanished.

The lake was larger than she'd expected, larger than it looked in the pictures her father had shown her when he was selling her on the move. Staring at it through the sun-glazed windshield made it seem somehow unreal, a projection from a different world made entirely of contrasting blues, a canvas of water and sky.

Jimmy had pulled the car off the paved road a half-mile back, cut onto a broad dirt road leading into a dense cluster of trees. Carrie-Ann was on the cusp of being nervous – being trapped with a strange boy in the ever-darkening woods and all – when the dark green canopy abruptly vanished and the tall tunnel of trees gave way to cavernous open sky. The dirt road terminated into a gravel-covered parking lot at the edge of the calm surface of Sabbath Lake, after which the surrounding town was named. Jimmy pulled straight to the edge of the parking lot so they could stare at the water from the car, the warm apple-skin red leather sticking lightly to the backs of her bare legs.

"You want to get out? Walk around?" he said, fingers dancing on the steering wheel.

"Sure," she said, opening the door to a light breeze, the air warm but not as dense as it had been in the car.

They walked down a slight grass slope to a skinny stretch of coarse beach. She saw a few folks seated along the edge of the lake, small dots of dark color smudged against the rough sand.

It came to her then what had been nagging at her since their arrival. It was the *calm* of the place. There were no boats on the water, despite the docks dotted every few hundred yards. There were no swimmers in the shallows, no laughing kids on the beach. No sunbathers. The people here just seemed to be... watching.

"So, where is everyone?"

Jimmy strolled along the lake's edge, inches from where the still water lay dormant. She followed, hurried to his side as they walked. "What do you mean?" he said.

"It's Saturday afternoon. It must be eighty degrees. A perfect day for a swim, don't you think?"

"Sure," he agreed, watching his feet.

"So... why isn't anyone swimming?"

He stopped, his head tilted, as if thinking, then those blue eyes fell on hers. A small smile played on his lips, but he seemed to fight it off. A look you had when trying not to laugh at someone. To spare their feelings, perhaps. "Ah," was all he said, then turned to face the lake.

"Are there no fishermen in Sabbath?" she teased.

When he didn't answer, she turned to the lake as well. Across the water she saw miniature houses with toy cars in their driveways; tiny people watering lawns or seated on back porches. The lake itself, she noticed, was free of waves, almost solid-looking. As if frozen. The water, although blue, looked black as sodden soot toward the middle, gradually darkening as the bottom fell away beneath.

"It's not the biggest lake in the world," he said. "But I'll tell you what. It's deep."

He put a hand on her elbow, and she nearly flinched at his touch. His fingers, long and firm, pressed into her skin; not painfully, but forcefully, as if he were about to guide her to the water's edge and shove her down into the shallows. She wondered, almost hysterically, if she should pull away, rebuke him. In the end, surprise and logic eclipsed anger and fear, and she stayed perfectly still, almost curious to see what would happen next.

"Anyway," he said, dropping his hand, his voice cheerful once more, "you'll find out all about the lake once you live here for a while. You'll come to love it, just like we all do." He turned and walked abruptly away, up the weathered grass and toward the parking lot. "Come on, Carrie-Ann," he said loudly, not turning back, "afternoon's a wastin'!"

She nodded, but found herself transfixed by the water. Yes, she could sense it now. How very deep it was.

As she stared, a moving cloud must have sprung free and drifted across the sky to blot the sun, for an enormous shadow passed along the water's surface. She looked to the sky, but saw nothing that might have created such an effect. When she looked once more at the lake, the shadow was gone.

She turned to go and noticed a small cluster of people seated a few hundred yards away at the top edge of the beach. She could have sworn they were all staring straight at her, their faces placid as the water, pale as foam.

Gooseflesh broke out on her arms and legs. She put her head down and walked quickly after Jimmy, doing her best not to run.

—§§—

The afternoon sun was waning, there were hints of red at the horizon, and Carrie-Ann was getting hungry. She'd never admit this, of course, not unless she wanted Jimmy to think her a cow.

The Chrysler cruised smoothly along the lakefront. Carrie-Ann caught blinks of blue where the trees thinned, then vanished altogether, the lake flashing into full view, exposing its naked splendor to all comers. She turned away, saw the road to downtown slip by on their left, but Jimmy never lifted his foot.

"Where now?" she said, trying to sound nonchalant but growing tired and irritated, which was unlike her. Something about the way the people at the lake had looked at her, something about the stillness of that massive body of water...

She sighed heavily, then caught herself, embarrassed for her own rudeness, even if it was only in her head.

But Jimmy just turned and smiled at her with those brilliant teeth and sparkling eyes. "We're heading out of town a ways, then we'll come back, hit main street and grab a bite to eat. Sound good?"

"Sure," she said, watching the white dashes of the road slip beneath them like Morse code, snatched up by the powerful engine. $S - O - S$, she thought, for no good reason at all.

—§§—

She saw it from the distance. Drab heaps of metal columned against the horizon, an expanse as disproportionate to her reality as the lake was. A large, surprisingly clean metal sign was strung up by heavy chain between two wooden posts the size of telephone poles. Jimmy slowed the car and turned to go beneath, stopped in the shadow of the creaking sign overhead.

"Riley's?" she said, looking up to read the name printed in large yellow letters against a rust-red metal backdrop.

"Yup, this is one of our star attractions here at Sabbath," Jimmy said, humor in his voice. "Folks come from miles around to visit old man Riley's, check out the soaring vistas, explore the rugged terrain, search for buried treasures."

She looked at him, gawping. His face stayed rigid for a moment, then he burst out laughing, and she with him. Carrie-Ann fought to compose herself, but Jimmy was busting more than one gut at her reaction.

"But it's a junkyard!" she said, too loudly, her laughter spilling out among the words.

"Yeah, sure it is. But *what* a junkyard."

She opened the door of the car and stepped out, looked at the seemingly endless acres of piled cars, metal, toilet seats and bicycles; at things so rusted up and run together it was nearly indistinguishable where one thing ended and another began. *Good Lord,* she thought, *how does a small town accumulate so much garbage?*

The flattened cars were stacked forty, fifty-feet high, the mountainous heaps of debris at least half that and twice as wide. A narrow dirt road twisted through the massive piles, like a path leading to a mystical land where everything was broken and rusted; an extinct civilization where only jagged ruins remained, massive paperweight reminders of a dead race.

"I've never seen so much crap in all my life," she said, amused at her own vulgarity. "My god Jimmy, look how high it goes. I wouldn't be surprised if there was a whole city underneath all that stuff, hidden from human eyes. I bet the dumps in Chicago aren't nearly as big."

He laughed, and she could feel him watching her. But she kept her eyes on the towers. *A wonderland of shit*, she thought, keeping *that* vulgarity to herself.

"You know, there's a story..." he said. "Well, it's gonna sound crazy."

"Tell me," she said, not knowing – not *really* – whether she wanted to hear the story or not.

"It's kind of an urban legend," he said, "that there's a car down there, way deep in the yard, sitting all by itself. An old Ford or something. It's rusted right through, big holes in the roof, in the hood. It's got wheels but no tires, and it's missing a door, and all the glass is broken out. But what's really weird is the car's color – as it first was, I mean. They say it's painted a bottomless, empty black. Dark as outer space." He paused, as if reflecting. "The kids like to say the car was built in hell. Crazy, right?"

"Geez," she said, scanning the piles of cars.

"What's really scary about this car," he continued, "even though it's junked and old and useless... well, it's said that anyone who dares sit inside of it..."

She looked at him, eyes wide. "What?"

His soft smile was amused, but his eyes had that hard look again. The look of ice so frozen it could never be thawed. He stepped behind her, lay his long fingers over her shoulders.

"They never come out," he whispered into her ear as she looked on at the broken towers of metal, the vast field of a used past. "A few kids *have* disappeared over the years," he said. "More than a few, actually. And lots of us hear rumors about dares and stupid stuff like that, stories about how kids like to go into Riley's to hunt for that car, dare each other to sit inside and see, see if anything happens. And *something* must have happened, right? Something pretty terrible. Because those kids, the ones that went looking for that old rusty Ford, the ones who found it, who sat inside... they never came back. Not ever."

Carrie-Ann noticed the reddening sun peek at her through the columns of junked autos and suddenly wanted to cry. An ache had settled into her guts like a cancer. She didn't know why, maybe it was the thought of those kids who had disappeared. Or maybe it was just hitting her, full-force, that this was her *home* now, and these were the highlights. The day was almost gone, and what had they made of it? A creepy lake and a haunted junkyard. She wondered if she'd ever be happy again.

"Say, I have a thought," he said, breaking her train of dark thoughts.

"Jimmy..."

"Let's give it a try."

She spun to look at him, saw his wide grin, his flickering eyes, his sculpted hair coming loose. A greasy strand hung over his face like a scythe.

"Try what?"

"To find it!" he said, grabbing one of her hands so tightly she winced. "We can try and find the car together. See, I think it's a portal, you know?" he said excitedly, his words pouring out of him in a rush. "Like a doorway, between this world and another. Only, you can only go one-way, or maybe not, but maybe when you come back... when you come back it's another time. The future, maybe... or the past! We'd leave and maybe never come back. Not ever. Can you imagine, Carrie-Ann?"

Carrie-Ann could imagine, and more than ever she wanted this day to end. She pulled her hand away, not as forcefully as she might have, but enough to wipe the smile from his face. "Jimmy, you're scaring me."

She turned away from him, looked down at her shoes. *What a mess*, she thought.

"Come on, Carrie-Ann, I was just joking," he said to her bowed head, and she thought he sounded sincere enough. She felt hands rest lightly on her hips and pushed down the rising thrill of his familiarity. He turned her to face him. "It's just a dumb story, okay? I was only fooling around."

She nodded, but said nothing, couldn't meet his eyes.

"Tell you what?" he said brightly, "Let's get out of here. We'll head back to town, get some food, then I'll take you home so you can get your room set up before bedtime, okay?"

She *was* hungry now, and getting very tired. "I guess," she said.

"Good," he said, sounding relieved. "Then come on, there's one more thing I want to show you."

She followed, somewhat petulantly, but was glad to go. She twisted her head for one last look at the junkyard, squinted at a dark shape hunched atop a stack of faraway cars. She imagined wings wider than the car it rested upon unfurl from its core and spread against the backdrop of hazy red sun before the dense shadow dropped away, disappeared into the eroded world beyond.

How strange are the shadows here, she thought, then settled into the warm seats of the convertible, reminded of the fabled old Ford that made children vanish, a doorway to other worlds.

They parked at the corner of Aylesbury and Dean street in the heart of downtown Sabbath. The Chrysler trembled, then went still.

The streetlights popped on as they got out of the car, the glow of the bulbs rising from brown to beige to white as they walked along the broad sidewalk. She had her sweater on now; the sun was gone and the evening had grown cold and surprisingly damp. The streets were quiet, nearly empty. In the distance she thought she heard the lapping of waves from the lake, and wondered if the stillness of the watery expanse had finally been curdled by the wind, re-animated by nature.

Dean Street was wide and glistening, the lamps fully amped against the misty evening encroaching upon them, the small stores that lined each side of the street well-lit, although most were closed. A flower shop, a bakery, a clothing store, a bank. The young couple passed beneath the shadow of a theater marquee and she eyeballed the darkened poster stretched behind glass on the side of the lobby entrance, but didn't recognize the image, or the title. The words seemed like gibberish. *Perhaps a foreign film,* she thought, but couldn't fathom it in such a small town. The poster was blotted with vague, intense imagery, as if it might be a horror film, or a monster movie.

They passed by and she didn't look back.

They approached the stark white window of a small drugstore. Bright white letters that hung against the brown brick façade read DOOGAN'S, the name bordered by a thin double-band of red-striped neon.

"How about a burger and a malted, on me?" Jimmy said, and Carrie-Ann just nodded, too exhausted now to argue or discuss. She was growing more and more depressed. She missed home. Not the house waiting for her a few short blocks away – the bedroom of blank walls and boxes, with curtains framing windows to a world she did not recognize – but *home.* Chicago. Her friends, the house she grew up in, the neighbors whose names she knew like the back of her hand. Safety.

"Here we are," he said cheerfully, and opened the door for her.

She stepped inside, blinded by fluorescent light. There was a row of small booths set into a clean white wall to her left, and a long counter to her right, lined along its length by red-backed swivel chairs. It reminded her, in a way, of Chicago, of the fountain shop she and her friends gathered at when they were younger, although it was much busier than this one.

This one was nearly empty.

One of the booths to her left harbored a morose-looking younger couple, and there were only two people sitting at the counter. She saw the Pharmacy sign hung against a sleek wood-paneled wall in the back, the word CLOSED hung on a rope triangle above a boarded-up window. Behind the counter stood a very tall man, his face white as egg yolk beneath a paper hat. He had a tiny bowtie at his neck and an apron around his bony hips. He held what looked like an ice cream scooper in one hand while the other rested on the counter in front of a teenage boy with ginger hair and freckles.

Both turned to look when Jimmy and Carrie-Ann entered, the bells strung to the heavy glass door stung the air, ringing their arrival.

"Here, sit down, Carrie-Ann," Jimmy said, and she did, right next to the teenage boy with freckles. "This here's Fred," he said, indicating the man behind the counter, "and Fred will get you whatever you want, won't you, Fred?"

"Sure I will," Fred said, nodding to Carrie-Ann and smiling through his putty face. "Always happy to welcome a new family to the neighborhood. How are you enjoying Sabbath so far, young lady?"

"It's fine," she said, trying to smile but feeling weak and out of sorts. "Just fine."

Fred smacked his hand lightly on the counter. "You look a little pale. Has Jimmy not been feeding you?"

She gave a wan smile. "He's been showing me the sites." She shifted her eyes to the right, saw the boy with freckles staring at her intently, and looked back to Fred. "I admit, I'm a little undernourished," she said, trying to sound light about it so as not to hurt Jimmy's feelings.

"I have just the thing," Fred said. "House special, and it's on me."

Someone clicked on a jukebox she must have missed when they entered and a crooning voice floated through the room. Fred turned away, grabbed a large metal cup, and began to pump white syrup into it from a steel sprocket.

She swiveled her seat to look behind her. The couple in the booth were watching her, and she noticed they were drinking what appeared to be vanilla milkshakes.

Feeling queasy, she turned back to watch Fred do his work.

He dolloped in a scoop of ice cream from a freezer before moving the metal cup beneath the spout of a massive keg which sprang directly from the wall. She watched as he turned the nozzle and carbonated water flooded in. He turned off the water and jammed the cup under a mixer, let it roar for a minute, then poured the thick wet shake into a tall ridged glass.

"Jimmy..." she said.

Fred dropped a long spoon into the glass then put the drink on the counter in front of her; a square red napkin nestled beneath, catching the perspiration.

Carrie-Ann looked down into the white, frothy shake. Bubbles rose and popped along its surface, and when the smell of it hit her she thought – she *knew* – it smelled like the lake. She thought the bubbles looked like eyes.

"What kind is it?" she asked, trying to keep her voice steady.

Fred, both hands on the counter, smiled as best he could, a crooked thing that cut into his face, making his eyes shift unnaturally. "That's a hometown special, young lady. Cream and syrup that's made right here in town, and water straight from Sabbath Lake itself. Carbonated, of course." He gave her a grotesque wink. "That's what makes it tickle."

She looked around for... she didn't know what. For help? For guidance? All eyes were on her, and the jukebox had switched songs and was playing Rag Mop. She tilted her head to Jimmy, spoke quietly to avoid a scene.

"Jimmy," she said under her breath, her eyes no higher than his strong chin. "I just want to go home."

"We will, angel," he said, "but first have something for the road. I'm telling you, Fred here is the best soda jerk in the county."

She looked back at Fred, his smile now gone.

"That's a hometown special," he repeated, as if surprised she didn't understand. "Once you drink that, you'll want nothing else. That there's a big cold glass of coming home."

She looked down at the shake, saw something the width of a spaghetti noodle slither along the surface then dip down into the rich contents of the glass and disappear. She put a hand to her mouth, turned and cried out despite herself, "I'd like to go home now!"

Jimmy put a hand on her shoulder, squeezed it lightly. "Yeah, sure, Carrie-Ann, no problem," he said flatly. "You must not be feeling well."

"No, I guess I'm not," she said. Relief flooded through her and she started to rise.

Jimmy slid his hand from her shoulder to her neck at the same instant Fred pulled her drink back toward his side of the counter. Jimmy's hand reached into her blond bob of hair and gripped it with a fierce tightness. She started to scream when he jumped to his feet, still clutching the back of her head, and slammed her face onto the hard countertop.

Carrie-Ann felt her nose crunch. White light exploded in her head.

Jimmy tugged her head back, then rammed it down onto the rock-solid countertop once more, harder this time than the last. Her mouth and chin took the brunt of it and her thoughts became blurred steam, drifting away from her like dead memories.

He pulled her head off the counter, cursing. Her eyes rolled wildly and her nose was bent. Blood covered her mouth and her chin and the countertop where her trembling hands spasmed. Jimmy wrenched her hair back with a hard twist so that she found herself looking at the ceiling. A slow-turning fan faced her, the blades spinning rhythmically to the song from the jukebox. She groaned and was surprised to find herself gagging on a dislodged tooth.

"Give it here," she heard Jimmy say, and she wondered why no one was helping her. Wondered why they were all just sitting there, watching. As the shock abated, the realization of her great danger flooded into her and she began to squirm, to wrestle from his grasp.

Strong hands grabbed her wrists, held them tight. *The freckled boy,* she thought.

Her hair was yanked back even harder. She winced and cried out. A calloused hand gripped her jaw and squeezed painfully until she opened wide.

She felt the cold, frothy shake being poured into her mouth, coating her tongue, pushing against the back of her throat. Reflexively, she gagged, hacked it out, then, almost convulsively, began to swallow. The taste was chalky and sweet and mixed with the tang of her own blood. The flavors exploded in her mouth, numbed her senses, and swam down into her.

The hand on her head released her hair and she was allowed a breath. The fingers on her jaw lightened. She stared up at the fan – dared not look away – as she felt the rush of the drink settle inside her stomach, begin to spread through her.

A tickle at the back of her brain almost made her smile.

"More," she said, and Jimmy, holding her head gently now, supportively, emptied the rest of the shake into her mouth.

She gulped it down.

Doorways in her mind burst open and her consciousness folded outward like the petals of a black flower as big and ethereal as the universe itself, as a thousand universes. In her mind's eye she soared among ancient ruins buried beneath a façade of rusted metal, inhabited by winged guardians and sleeping gods. She flew past and dove deep, deep into the lake, past the white god that slept there, slid along the edge of the great bubble, then passed beyond.

I am the gateway.

The words echoed in her mind as she blasted past galaxies and hit light speed, spinning into an endless abyss of stardust flesh, a million worlds at her fingertips.

Then, with a blinding flash of light and a thunderous *CRACK,* she slammed abruptly back into her flesh. Her body convulsed and fell from the swivel chair, landed hard on the clean linoleum floor, writhing. Blood and white cream sprayed from her mouth and nose as the kids watched in silence. After a minute, the convulsions stopped, her body went limp.

Jimmy knelt down, put a towel to her chin, wiped a tear from her broken face.

"How do you feel?" he asked.

She smiled back, her mouth smeared in blood, a new root already climbing from the gum where a tooth had been knocked free. She felt the bones of her nose shift and click into place, and her eyes, she knew, were bright as his own. "Fine," she whispered, and he helped her to her feet. People on the sidewalk stood watching through the window. She looked at all the faces and knew them. She turned to Jimmy, her mind a buzzing hive of voices, and slipped a hand into his.

He squeezed it reassuringly. "What now?"

"Now?" she said, as if waking from a sweet dream. "Now..."

She wiped blood from her chin, hungrily licked the last of the white froth from her lips. She smiled like a serpent, like Eve.

"Now it's time to go home."

About the Author

Philip Fracassi, an author and screenwriter, lives in Los Angeles. He is the author of the novellas *Fragile Dreams, Sacculina,* and *Shiloh*. His debut collection, *Behold The Void*, is available in print, audio and eBook. His feature film, *Girl Missing*, is currently on demand via iTunes and Amazon.

His stories have been printed in numerous magazines and anthologies including *Dark Discoveries, Cemetery Dance* and *The Best Horror of the Year (Volume Ten)*.

You can visit his website at pfracassi.com or find him via social media on Facebook, Instagram (pfracassi) and Twitter (@philipfracassi).

ALSO FROM
LOVECRAFT EZINE PRESS

The Endless Fall, by Jeffrey Thomas

Whispers, by Kristin Dearborn

Nightmare's Disciple, by Joseph S. Pulver, Sr.

Autumn Cthulhu, edited by Mike Davis

The Lurking Chronology, by Pete Rawlik

The Sea of Ash, by Scott Thomas

The King in Yellow Tales volume I,
by Joseph S. Pulver, Sr.

Blood Will Have Its Season, by Joseph S. Pulver, Sr.

The Peaslee Papers, by Peter Rawlik

*Carnacki: The Edinburgh Townhouse
and Other Stories,* by William Meikle

Made in the USA
Middletown, DE
09 June 2019